# Wild Bird

A NOVEL

LEANNE BAUGH

Red Deer Press

Published in Canada by Red Deer Press, 195 Allstate Parkway, Markham, ON L3R 4T8

Published in the United States by Red Deer Press, 311 Washington Street, Brighton, MA 02135



Red Deer Press acknowledges with thanks the Canada Council for the Arts and the Ontario Arts Council for their support of our publishing program. We acknowledge the financial support of the Government of Canada through the Canada Book Fund (CBF) for our publishing activities.

Edited for the Press by Peter Carver
Text and cover design by Tanya Montini
Proudly printed in Canada by Houghton Boston

**Library and Archives Canada Cataloguing in Publication**
Title: Wild bird / Leanne Baugh.
Names: Baugh, Leanne, 1959- author.
Description: First edition.
Identifiers: Canadiana 20200363018 | ISBN 9780889956360 (softcover)
Subjects: LCGFT: Novels.
Classification: LCC PS8603.A8977 W55 2021 | DDC jC813/.6—dc23

**Publisher Cataloging-in-Publication Data (U.S.)**
Names: Baugh, Leanne, 1959-, author.
Title: Wild Bird / Leanne Baugh.
Description: Markham, Ontario : Red Deer Press, 2021.| Summary: "Kate Harding at 16 rebels against the social norms of the remote colonial town of Victoria in 1861. Here, Indigenous people are regarded as fodder for the small pox epidemic, and Kate's hope of practicing medicine is disparaged. But she is determined and eventually wins out." -- Provided by publisher.
Identifiers: ISBN 978-0-88995-636-0 (paperback)
Subjects: LCSH Smallpox—Juvenile fiction. | Indigenous people — Canada -- Juvenile fiction. | Families -- Juvenile fiction. | Friendship – Juvenile fiction.| BISAC: JUVENILE FICTION / Social Themes / Self-Esteem & Self-Reliance.
Classification: LCC PZ7.B746Be |DDC [F] – dc23

www.reddeerpress.com

*For my mom and my sister*

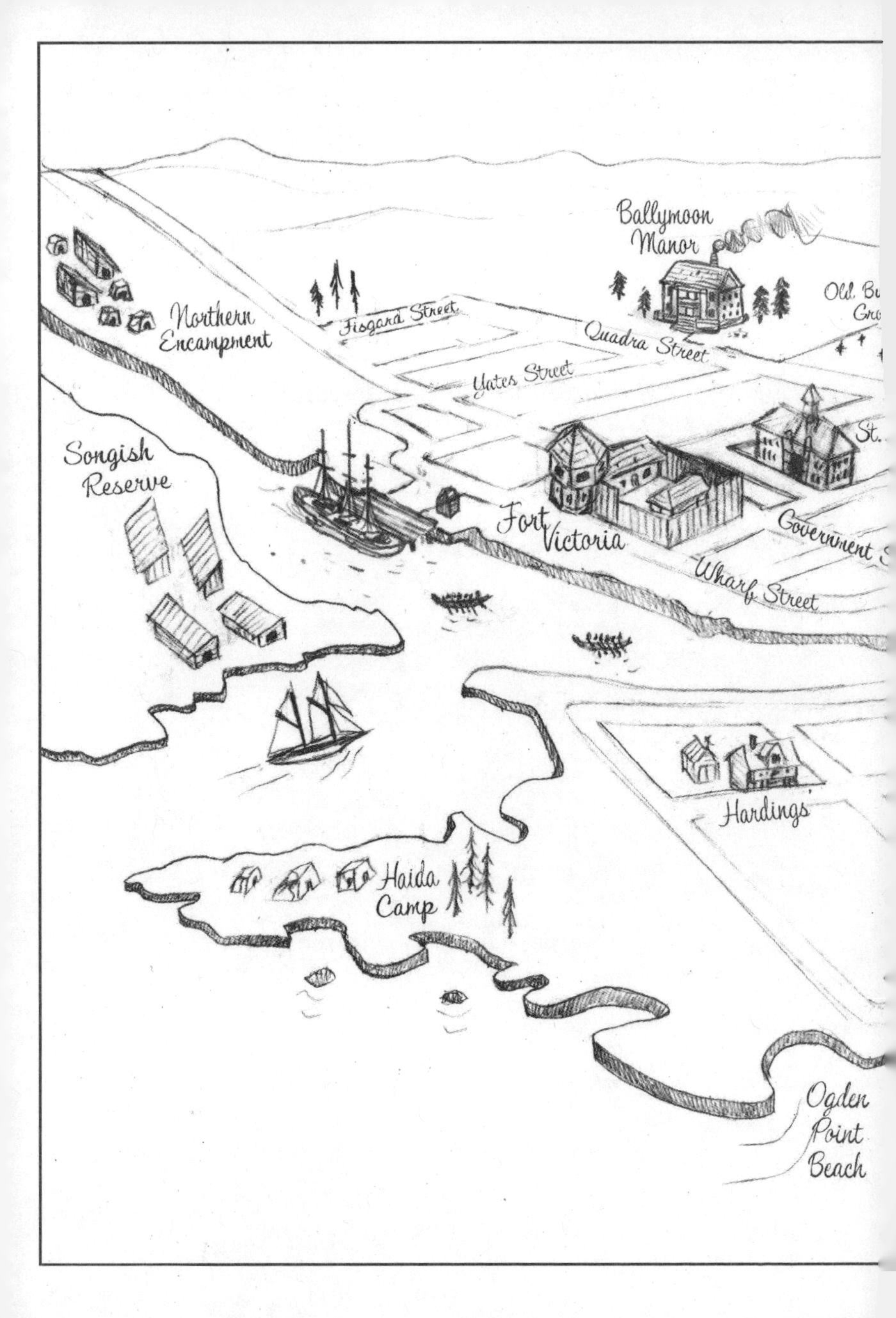
Ballymoon
Manor
Northern
Encampment
Fisgard Street
Quadra Street
Yates Street
Songish
Reserve
Fort
Victoria
Government
Wharf Street
Hardings
Haida
Camp
Ogden
Point
Beach

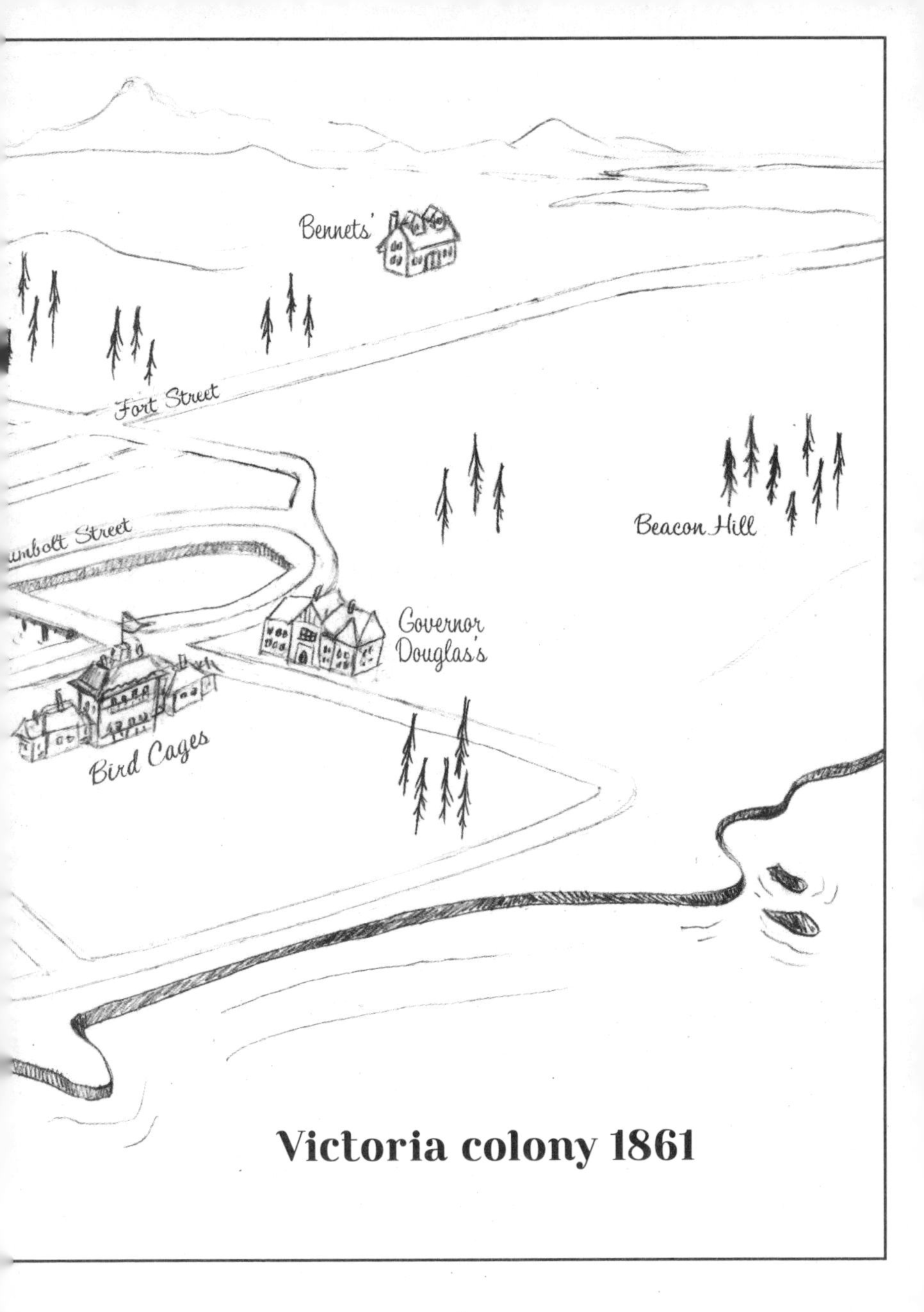


**Victoria colony 1861**

# Chapter 1

## Victoria, Colony of Vancouver Island, November 1861

Kate's mama writhes in pain on the bed, covers thrown off. Her anguished scream shoots a violent shiver up Kate's spine.

"Annie!" Kate yells.

The housemaid rushes into the room. Her reddish curls stick out of the frilly white maid's cap that has slipped to one side, her apron streaked where she wiped blood off her hands after changing the bed sheets.

"Governor and Lady Douglas must be back by now. Go quickly." Panicked, Kate stuffs a sheet between her mama's legs to staunch the flow.

Annie stands frozen and wide-eyed, watching the blood soak the sheet.

"Go!"

Annie spins around and hurries out of the room.

Mama moans, her head moving from side to side. She's losing consciousness.

Kate takes her hand, feels around for a pulse, like she has seen her papa do. The heartbeat is faint and irregular, which makes Kate's heart pound even harder. The mound on Mama's stomach looks smaller under the thin linen nightdress—as if the baby is disappearing before her eyes. Why would Mama put herself through this again, and so soon? She wrings out a wet cloth and gently wipes Mama's face, that is red with blotches and covered in sweat.

Mama looks up at Kate with dread in her eyes.

"This baby. It's too early, Katherine." She lets out a cry. "Much too early."

"All will be well, Mama." But her voice is shaky, unconvincing; surely not the comforting tone Mama needs to hear. "I've sent Annie for Lady Douglas."

"Where is your papa? He should be here. William ... always leaving ... always away ..." She lets out another painful shriek.

"He will be here as soon as he's able."

When *will* Papa arrive back? He left at dawn by canoe with two Cowichan men to amputate some poor man's gangrenous leg, something the Indian doctor refuses to do. Between contractions, her mama lies limp. Kate places another log in the fireplace and then goes to the window;

she pushes aside the heavy green brocade drapes to let in more light. Although it's only mid-afternoon, the sky is dark as coal—the color of her mood. Rain pounds on the window, obscuring a clear view, but she can still make out the ghostly forms of ships at anchor in the harbor. This weather will surely slow Papa's return, which will only prolong the agony for Mama.

She picks up a candle from the chest of drawers, catching her reflection in the mirror hanging above. She looks older than her sixteen years. Dark gray lines are etched under her tense eyes, her wavy black hair as wild as ever, sticking up every which way, but she doesn't care enough to pin it back. She trims the candlewick and lights one of the two candles on either side of Mama's bed. The smell of wax makes her feel warm. Although it already feels like nightfall, she'll wait for dark to light the other to ration the expensive wax.

At the bedroom door, her small brother James moves the arms of a wooden redcoat toy soldier. He flinches when their mama cries out in pain. Kate goes to him.

"Back to your room, that's a good boy. Annie will be back soon."

"Is Mama going to die?" His little brow furrows and his face is drained of color.

She bends down and looks into his big eyes, so full of fear and, like hers, sapphire blue. She cups his freckled cheeks. "I will fetch you soon to meet your new baby brother or sister." Kate gently guides him out of the room.

"I hope it's a baby boy, so I can show him how to shoot an arrow from my new bow, and ride my wooden pony when he's a bigger boy like me. I will sing him nursery rhymes—'Bye, baby Bunting, Father's gone a-hunting, Mother's gone a-milking, Sister's gone a-silking ...'"

"Off you go, now."

James saunters down the hallway, still reciting the rhyme. "... Brother's gone to buy a skin, to wrap the baby Bunting in."

Mama continues to moan but moves less and less. Kate replaces the sopping sheet with another. Feels numb. Helpless. If only she knew what to do, maybe she could save Mama and possibly the new infant. She sits in a chair by the bed and holds Mama's hand, which rests limp in hers. Out the window, streams of rain race down the glass.

After what feels like an eternity, Kate hears the clop-clopping of horses' hooves outside, and sees the Douglas's carriage splashing through the deep puddles in the road. Soon there are footsteps on the stairs.

Lady Douglas, the governor's wife and one of the colony's midwives, enters the room, her clothing swooshing around her. She quickly removes her gloves, bonnet, and coat, and throws them on a chair. "Annie is fetching the water," she says to Kate in her halting English. And then to the patient, "I am here now, Louisa." Lady Douglas first looks into her face, then removes the blood-soaked sheet. Kate watches how she examines Mama, feels her belly for the baby.

"We can be thankful it's not in breech position," she tells Kate.

"Breech?"

"When the baby's buttocks or feet want to come first. If baby is not headfirst, it is a harder, more painful birth. And often fatal."

"Amelia." Mama grabs Lady Douglas's hand. "Not now ... not again," she gasps.

"Babies come in their own time." Lady Douglas pats her hand. "The head is already crowning."

Kate is sure it *is* happening again. She was just four years old when baby John made a hasty entry into this world in England, where her family lived at the time. His face was as shriveled as an old man's and as pale as the white blanket in which he was wrapped. Kate had every confidence his tiny limp body could be nudged back to life. Like when she found a goldfinch lying motionless on the ground outside her window. She and her older brother Arthur had knelt down beside it, watched it closely as it began to move little by little, until it righted itself. It splayed and flapped its yellow and black wings before it eventually flew away.

When baby John refused to be willed back to life, Kate was shattered.

One year later, Charlotte was also born too early and sickly. And although Kate breathed into her face and gently held her fingers, tiny as baby worms, Charlotte lived only six months. After burying baby Charlotte, Kate vowed she would not allow one more Harding baby to die.

Not long after they arrived on Vancouver Island, James came into the world; his robust cries echoed throughout the house. It was a joyous sound, compared to the gasps and whimpers of her other newborn siblings. Kate was determined not to lose this baby brother, and she vigilantly stood watch over him, refusing to let him slip out of life too early.

A year later, there was another baby, named Louisa after Mama, because of her full head of black hair that she and Kate had inherited from their mother. Even though Louisa was born dead, Kate was ripped apart with guilt that instead of standing watch, she had slept through the birth. If she had only stayed awake long enough to greet her baby sister into this world, she would have lived.

Although Kate knows she had no influence over her baby siblings' life or death, she is still haunted. What special dispensation from the heavens allowed Arthur, James, and herself to be born alive—and stay alive?

Annie enters with mud caked on the bottom of her skirt. With her spindly arms, she struggles to carry a bucket of steaming water and place it by the bed. Lady Douglas rolls up the sleeves of her black silken blouse. From inside her large black bag, she pulls out an apron and soap. Wraps the apron around her and washes her hands and arms, right up to her elbows. She hands Kate the soap. "The placenta may be disengaged. Baby must be delivered soon."

"Go to James, Annie," Kate says, as she lathers her hands with the soap. Annie takes one more horrified look at the bloody bed before she leaves the room.

While Kate scrubs her hands and arms, she wishes she knew what a placenta was. Maybe she could have reengaged it, somehow. Stopped the bleeding. Lady Douglas sops up more blood between Mama's legs.

After several more excruciating contractions, a tiny

withered body slides into Lady Douglas's hands. "Another daughter, Louisa."

"Will this one live?" Mama's voice is soft and weak.

"That I cannot tell." Lady Douglas knows loss all too well. Of the thirteen children she gave birth to, only four survived to adulthood.

Kate carefully watches how Lady Douglas first places two clamps on the long white spiraling cord, and then uses special scissors to sever in between. She then holds up the baby for Kate to wrap in a blanket. Her baby sister is light as a kitten. The blood-streaked skin is purple and wrinkled. Kate watches as the placenta is delivered—a round bloody mass that looks like an enormous cow's liver. The cord is attached at its center. It is both repulsive and intriguing that this organ is birthed along with the baby. Kate wonders what purpose it serves. And how such a mass exists with a baby inside the womb. She takes the tiny baby to her mother.

"Here she is, Mama." Her mother peers at the baby, who looks more reptile than human, turns her head away, and shuts her eyes tightly. Mama refuses to hold her baby daughter, even for a moment. Aren't a mother's arms where an infant should breathe its last breath?

Late into the evening, shadows dance on the walls and ceiling from the flickering candles. Mama sleeps soundly, while Kate rocks the baby in the chair her grandmother sent from England when James was born. The only movement is the tiny chest heaving, gasping for every breath. A deep sadness washes over Kate, who knows not even Papa can save this wee one.

She hears the front door thump closed and Annie's high-pitched voice, full of emotion. Footsteps rumble up the stairs and her father rushes into the room.

"Thank God you're home, Papa."

He goes directly to Mama's bedside. "How is she?" Even with his height and sturdy frame, Kate thinks he moves so gracefully, as if his feet barely even touch the ground.

"She lost a considerable amount of blood. Lady Douglas stayed until she settled."

Mama doesn't wake when he caresses her head. Kate aches for Papa when she sees the guilt pulling down his shoulders, like she's seen so many times before when he feels he's failed.

"There were no signs the baby was coming before you left, Papa." He takes the baby from Kate, unwraps the blanket, and holds the wee thing that fits in just one of his large hands.

"There was nothing to be done." He doesn't need to examine the baby to know she will not live out the night.

"Did your mama give her a name?"

Kate shakes her head.

"Her name will be Violet, after my mama." He wraps the baby up again and sits with her on a chair beside Mama's bed.

In Kate's bedroom, the relentless rain still hammers the window as she looks out into the night. Dogs howl at the faint drumming and chanting from the Songish village across the harbor.

Even though the candle has almost burned right down, she sits at her desk and picks up a small photo of Arthur, with his serious eyes and thick wavy hair. She wonders if the color has stayed auburn all these years, or has it turned darker brown? She traces his image with her finger before putting the photograph down. Reaching into a drawer, she takes out a sheet of paper, dips her pen in the inkwell.

*2 Nov 1861*

*Dearest Arthur,*

*What kind of cruel God would take yet another infant from an already grieving mother? Mama only recently recovered from baby Louisa's passing, and now Violet, born only hours ago, gasps for her every breath, and will soon be the latest casualty. In Mama's world, bearing children is the most important and noble role for a woman. And although three of her children have survived, it seems she cannot forgive herself for ones who did not.*

*I cannot endure the next months of mourning and melancholy; the color black is most dreadful on the eyes. But Mama will exempt me from wearing mourning attire, as the drab, miserable color will most definitely not attract a suitor that she hopes for me. How fortunate you are that, for the past seven years, you have been sheltered from this death and misery. But how unfortunate for me that you and I have been apart. I move about life feeling like I have a limb missing. Your letters are what keep my sanity intact.*

*Your last letter was full of museums and galleries. You know how I love when you write in great detail about what you are studying at St. George's, following in our father's footsteps. I re-read those letters over and over again. I especially like hearing about the surgery theater, where I imagine you and your fellow medical students looking on as your professor carves into a cadaver.*

*Tell me something cheery about life in London. I only have my faint childhood memories to rely on.*

*Forever yours,*

*K*

# Chapter 2

A beam of sun pours through the brooding clouds, lighting the Old Burying Ground east of town, but leaving the rest of Victoria in darkness. Reverend and Mrs. Fleming lead the funeral cortège, next her father, then Annie holding James's hand. Kate follows, hiking up her skirt as she trudges down the path thick with mud. Mama, still weak from the difficult birth, missed the church funeral and stayed behind at the house to welcome guests after the interment.

"What will happen to baby Violet after she's put into the ground, Annie?" James says, too loud. "Will her body be eaten up by worms and maggots? And will her spirit fly right to heaven before she's buried or after?"

"Quiet down your chatter," Annie says. Kate thinks Annie's tone could have been gentler, under the circumstances.

Kate should have gone against Mama's wishes and worn her tall India rubber boots. Who would care what she wore on her feet at her baby sister's funeral? Instead, here she is in proper fashion, slipping and sloshing through the muck in her short leather boots, about to turn an ankle. She glances back. Only a few of the colony men make their way down the path, including Governor Douglas. So many funerals, no one can attend them all. To uphold tradition that deems women too delicate to witness a dead body being buried, their wives stay in their carriages while the men attend the interment. Kate has insisted on attending the burial of all her infant siblings.

Mr. Eamonn O'Brien glances over at her. Kate nods and immediately blushes. Usually his business interests would have whisked him away after the funeral at the church. But surely he would be here; her mother is determined to marry her off to this wealthy merchant almost twenty years her senior, who made his riches from Fraser Valley gold. Unlike her father's moustache, which is trimmed handsomely, Mr. O'Brien's is as red and bushy as a fox's tail, as is what little hair he has left on his head. But Kate finds herself drawn to his charm and warm smile. In a grove of trees, Mr. and Mrs. Johnson stand with their two small children. The Johnsons are one of the many Black families welcomed to Fort Victoria by Governor Douglas, to avoid discrimination in California. Kate went with her father to their small shack outside Fort Victoria's walls when their small son suffered a fractured arm. They have now moved into a fine house on Burdett Street, and the young patient has grown into a healthy, robust boy.

The tiny coffin sits next to the wide-open mouth of a grave, hungry for yet another Harding baby.

The Reverend Fleming begins his address: "Forasmuch as it hath pleased Almighty God of His great mercy to take unto Himself the soul of our dear baby Violet, here departed ...."

A twinge tugs at Kate's chest when she sees her father looking as sad as she's ever seen him.

"We therefore commit her body to the ground; earth to earth, ashes to ashes, dust to dust; in sure and certain hope of the Resurrection to eternal life, through our Lord Jesus Christ." The Reverend Fleming continues: "Who shall change our vile body that it may be like unto His glorious body, according to the mighty working, whereby He is able to subdue all things to Himself."

The coffin disappears into the ground. How could a baby who survived but six hours ever possess a vile body?

Horses whinny and stomp their feet as the men walk to carriages lined up and down Quadra and Meares Streets.

Before the Governor climbs into his carriage to join Lady Douglas, he offers his hand to Kate's father.

"My deepest condolences, William."

"Thank you for being here," Papa says. "Will you and Lady Douglas join us at our home?"

They won't, because Lady Douglas avoids social gatherings. Like her husband, she is of mixed race. Governor Douglas was born in British Guyana to a Scottish father and Creole mother. Lady Douglas has Cree and French blood. Her difficulty speaking the English language has made her very shy and awkward. She retires as much into the background as she possibly can. When necessary, her grown daughters are left to take over the social obligations.

"I am afraid the affairs of the state are pressing," Douglas says. "I set sail for New Westminster later today."

"Of course," Papa says, as the Governor tips his top hat and climbs into the carriage to join his wife. It was Governor Douglas who, seven years ago, lured Papa from the bustle of industrial London, England, to the wilds of Vancouver Island. After what felt like a lifetime at sea, Kate remembers sailing into Victoria Harbour to see Fort Victoria's bastion and palisades. There was little sign of human existence, which made Kate feel desperately lonely from that moment on.

Only a few mourners gather at the Harding home after the cemetery. Annie helped Kate move the furniture to the sitting room to make space, but it wasn't needed. Kate can see it in Mama's gaunt, pale face when she looks around the room, that she wished for more mourners. In Mama's mind, even a funeral is a social occasion in which success is measured by the number of guests in attendance. Annie offers a tray of dainty sandwiches to the guests, while Mrs. Fleming, the minister's wife, serves tea. Like a queen, Mama holds court as guests pay their respects.

The "throne" on which Mama sits is a large chair with ornately carved wood around the frame, legs, and armrests, the seat and backrest covered in red silk. It was bought from an auction house in England when times were better. Mama will never forgive Papa two things: first, his disastrous investment decision that drained the family's fortune to a fraction of what it once was. Money is still bleeding from the family's coffers to pay off creditors in England. The second unforgiveable act was, because of the humiliation, dragging her away from London society to "this godforsaken backwoods colony." Like Mama, Kate is plagued by a deep longing for life as it once was.

Dr. Helmcken, one of Fort Victoria's original doctors, sits in a corner, admiring his wife and two-year-old son. As a physician, he and his family lead a comfortable life. Being the son-in-law of the Governor must also have its financial benefits. But Kate isn't exactly sure what they might they be. If it weren't for servicing debt, the Hardings would surely be as well-to-do.

Fanny Applegate grabs Kate's hand and pulls her over to Emily Piper. Both graduated St. Ann's School with her last June. Emily is in the corner, stuffing a sandwich into her mouth. Her blouse, already terribly strained from holding her ample bosom, looks about to pop its buttons. The two girls are close to Kate's age, and both are affable and kind-hearted. But in terms of interests and passions, they could not be more different than her.

"Very sorry about your baby sister," Emily says as she takes another bite.

"Thank you for coming," Kate says. "I do appreciate it."

Quiet and solemn for a moment.

"Kate, you missed the most exquisite party," Fanny bursts out. "It was at Hillside Farm after the horse races."

"HMS *Constance* docked in Esquimalt harbor," Emily says, licking her fingers. "Full of handsome naval officers—"

“Who were very much in need of dance partners,” Fanny interjects.

“That party was the same night my mama was suffering in labor with my baby sister, who didn’t live out the night,” Kate says. “The thought of attending the party had not crossed my mind.” She regrets the biting tone of her voice—these girls are just trying to be friendly and they mean no harm.

They share a look. “So very sorry, Kate,” says Emily.

“No need to be sorry. It’s been a very sad and exhausting time, that’s all. If you will excuse me.” Loneliness gnaws at her insides as she turns and picks up a teacup and saucer from a tray. Try as she might to make meaningful connections, Kate has given up the pretence of ever having female companionship. She feels infinitely more comfortable in adult company, and moves across the room to where her father is in deep conversation with a group of men.

“Congratulations on your election win, Joseph,” her father says to Mr. Trutch.

“Thank you, William. We’ll see if I’m a political animal, after all. My business interests may keep me from the House of Assembly a great deal, but I still plan on serving my constituents.”

"What is the first order of business you hope to champion?" Mr. Pemberton asks.

"Indians must be relieved of as much land as possible, as soon as possible," Trutch says. "They really have no right to the lands they claim, nor are they of any actual value or utility to the land."

Papa pipes in, "But Douglas made it clear that once reserves were established, they were not to be reduced, either by the encroachment of individual settlers or by the collective action of the House of Assembly."

Flora Fleming, the minister's wife, joins the circle of men and pours tea into empty cups.

"Under the treaties, the Songish have surrendered their land entirely and forever in return for a few blankets," Trutch replies. "As the police superintendent, you well know, Pemberton, that they are utter savages living along this coast—drunkards and brawlers—committing murder and robbery amongst themselves, one tribe upon another, and on white people who trade with them. English law must be enforced at all costs."

Kate remembers the massacre that took place just north of town in Rock Bay two years ago, when Songish, Haida, Bella Bella, Cowichan, and other tribes went to battle against each other. Many were either slaughtered or wounded. Ever since, Kate has been afraid of how easily the violence could extend to White society that is greatly outnumbered by the natives.

"Surely you cannot include all tribes in your insinuation, Mr. Trutch," Mrs. Fleming says. "Our local Songish Indians have been nothing but peaceful and cooperative with English society, since the building of Fort Victoria almost two decades ago. And I daresay many colonists heavily rely on their labor."

Kate has known Mrs. Fleming to be an informed and intelligent woman, but she has never before witnessed her challenge male opinion. Kate feels uneasy, protective of Mrs. Fleming, wanting to pull her away from these men, who will most likely take exception to her confidence.

"As the wife of a minister, Mrs. Fleming, you must agree that not a single native can be considered to have attained even the most glimmering perception of the Christian creed."

"I would say to you, sir, that the Indians in my acquaintance demonstrate Christian values as much as, if not more than, many of the gold miners that have littered this city the past few years."

The men share a surprised look, as Mrs. Fleming fills up Papa's teacup and walks away. Kate can't help but be impressed by her poise and conviction.

Behind his hand, Trutch replies, “The local savages are the ugliest and laziest creatures, and we should as soon think of being afraid of our dogs as of them.” Some of the men chuckle. The shocked expression on Papa’s face mirrors Kate’s feelings.

“Mrs. Fleming is right to say there’s much to admire in the natives,” Papa says. “They are resourceful, bold, brave, and, for the most part, peaceful. Have civilized men much more to offer society?” He turns his back to the group to speak with Reverend Fleming.

“Nevertheless, they are still Indians,” says one of the men. The rest nod.

Mama firmly clutches Mr. O’Brien’s arm as they approach her. “Mr. O’Brien would like to pay his respects, Katherine.” She leaves her alone with him.

Kate curtseys. O’Brien bows and then holds out his hand to Kate.

“May I extend my deepest condolences to you, Katherine.” In the background, Kate sees Fanny and Emily watching with interest, and possibly envy. With his wealth and charm, Mr. O’Brien is considered one of the most desired suitors in Victoria. Kate has mixed feelings as she offers her hand.

“Kind of you to come, Mr. O’Brien.” The skin on his hand

feels too soft for a man, even one that isn't a laborer. Does he use lotions that a woman might use?

"I wouldn't miss an opportunity to support you and your family under these difficult circumstances." His gray eyes peer so deeply and intensely into hers, she has to look away. He pulls her closer to him. Kate can smell smoked fish on his breath. His bushy moustache tickles her cheek, and he whispers, "You are an angel."

"My family is grateful that you came." A warm blush washes over her face and down her neck as she slips out of his grip. "If you will excuse me, Mr. O'Brien." Flustered by his attentiveness, she picks up a tray and begins collecting empty cups and plates.

In the kitchen, she puts down the tray, while Annie pours hot water into the soapy dish pail. "How many are still here?" Annie asks as she delicately washes a teacup. "Do I need to put on more tea?"

"No, most have left. It is just clean-up now." Kate puts on an apron and begins drying the dishes.

She follows Annie's glance out the window. The golden afternoon sun lights up the horse barn, where Annie's young man Peter leans against the fence. A piece of straw sticks out of his mouth.

"How long has he been waiting?" Kate asks.

"Well over an hour."

"Wash the rest of these dishes—then off you go."

"Are you sure, Miss Kate?"

"You've been run off your feet today. I can finish up."

Annie glances at Kate with a smile as she scrubs a pot. "I saw that Mr. O'Brien is in attendance. Has he proposed to you yet?"

Kate shakes her head. "No."

"His manor on Quadra Street is so grand, according to my friend, Tilly. She was a housemaid there until she married."

Kate picks up another dish to dry. "I have not yet promised my hand to anyone."

"You are as beautiful as a princess, Miss Kate. If it is not Mr. O'Brien you marry, one day you will meet a man who loves you just like my Pete loves me."

Kate looks out the window where Peter feeds grass to Nora, their horse.

"There is something I need to tell you," Annie says, nervously picking up a glass bowl to wash. "I haven't had the heart to tell Mrs. Harding, considering all that she's gone through lately."

Kate knows what's coming. "Not you, too, Annie." Like

Helen and Margaret before her, Annie is leaving them.

"Pete purchased his miner's license and, after we marry, we'll set out for the gold fields in the Cariboo. Pete's heard the gold near Antler Creek is so close to the surface, you do not even have to dig for it."

"But, Annie, the gold fields are no place for a woman."

"I will not let him set off without me. I can be a great help, carrying supplies and cooking for him." Annie's tiny back could very well break, carrying a miner's huge sack.

"Then I wish you and Pete all the very best." Kate doubts Annie would be able to last even one day on the rustic trail, with such a rough and rowdy group of miners.

"I will give proper notice, Miss. Your family has been so very good to me. Especially you and Dr. Harding. And I will very much miss wee James."

It may be near impossible to replace Annie with the dire shortage of domestic help in Victoria. It's clear the running of the household will mostly fall on Kate's shoulders.

"Away you go before Pete takes back his proposal." Kate picks up a handful of cutlery to dry.

"Thank you, Miss Kate."

Annie takes her coat off the hook at the door and replaces it with her apron. She smiles at Kate, then opens the door.

Through the window, Kate watches her run across the field. Pete meets her halfway, scoops her up into his arms, and spins her in the air. They kiss for a long moment and make their way down the road, arm-in-arm. A longing stabs at Kate's chest. *Is it really possible to marry for love?*

The house is dark and quiet. Carrying a candle to light her way, Kate inhales deeply to take in the smell of sweet tobacco, and follows it to the back of the house, where her father has his doctor's surgery. When he isn't making calls to his patients' homes, he sees them here. She finds him here most nights, when James and Mama have gone to bed, alone and smoking his pipe. He is usually updating patient case notes in his thick book, but tonight he works through a stack of bills beside him, trying to balance the family finances.

"It is late, Papa."

"I could say the same to you, my dear." She wraps her arms around his shoulders and kisses his cheek. She then wanders around his office and opens a trunk full of medical tools: forceps, stomach pump, stethoscope, tourniquet, cupping instruments, and the amputation saw. She inspects his small leather container full of bottled medicines and tonics, which have intrigued her since she was a small child.

She turns to her father and sees his anxious brow furrow, as he enters another debt into the ledger.

"I have spoken to Sister Mary ..." she says, bracing herself for an argument.

"We have talked about this before, Kitty."

"But, Papa, she said she could pay me to teach a class of young students at St. Ann's."

"You know your mama believes it improper for you to work for money."

"But do you think it improper?"

"A young lady of a certain class should have no worries about working for money to support her family. She should be focused on domestic tasks alone."

"Even when her family is in need of money?"

Her father looks up; it's clear she's hurt his pride. But why is he so stubborn and unable to listen to reason? He taps the spent ashes from his pipe into a bowl and lays the pipe on his desk.

"What is to be my future, Papa? Marry into money, whether for love or not, just so the family will be looked after? Is that my lot in life?"

"Your mama and I wish only for your happiness."

"Being productive and helping pay the family bills would

make me very happy. I can see how this financial burden weighs on you."

He puts down his pen and slaps the ledger closed. "This discussion is over," he says sharply. She has pushed too far. He takes one of the candles from the desk and leaves.

She opens the ledger to see that the numbers in the expenditure column greatly outweigh the numbers in the income column.

# Chapter 3

Annie brings a tea tray into the sitting room, where Kate talks with Mrs. Fleming and Mama. Mama waits until Annie leaves the room and closes the door behind her.

"Annie has forced us into such a difficult situation. I have inquired extensively, and there are no domestic servants in need of work in all of Victoria. How are we expected to cope?"

"Annie is not leaving to vex you, Mama. She and Pete are marrying."

"Could that girl not have attracted a more stable, well-heeled young man, rather than one whose head is full of absurd notions? Taking Annie to the gold fields? Ludicrous! A proper road is yet to be built. She will not last but a day."

"Louisa, I do know of a young girl who might perfectly suit your situation," says Mrs. Fleming. Her light brown hair with its hint of red matches a stripe in her plaid dress.

"If you are thinking about that girl with the long pointy

nose, the Browns have hired her already. Besides, is she not Catholic?"

Kate pours the tea and says, "You don't seem to mind that Mr. O'Brien is both Catholic and Irish." She abhors her mother's hypocrisy.

"That is different. He is unlike most of his kind. He is both an ambitious and industrious man, who turned around his meagre circumstances to acquire much wealth. That is only to be admired."

Kate hands Mrs. Fleming her tea and they share a knowing look. "You were saying, Mrs. Fleming?"

"The girl's name is Lucy. She was the housemaid for the Gordons before they went back to Scotland, and the McIvors before that. Both families said she was not only a good worker but a bright, pleasant girl, as well." Mrs. Fleming takes a sip of tea and puts her cup down. "I first met Lucy when the Reverend Fleming and I visited the Songish Village."

"For heaven's sake, Flora," Mama says. Her black mourning dress against her pale complexion makes her face look even more severe. "I would rather have a dirty floor and no food on the table than an Indian living under my roof."

"Most Songish housemaids do not like to live away from their village," Mrs. Fleming says. "She would come each morning and leave when her work is done. As I said, the Gordons had only good things to say about her."

"Mama, if we are to hire a replacement for Annie, we may not have a choice. We cannot carry the burden of running this household on our own. Can we not just meet this Indian girl?"

Mama's face is tense as she picks up her teacup. "I would far rather hire an Irish girl—or even a Chinaman—over the Indian."

Kate walks Mrs. Fleming to the door. "The Reverend and I will be visiting the village later this week," Mrs. Fleming says. "I will arrange a meeting then."

"Thank you. I really do appreciate it, even though Mama has objections."

"Goodbye, Katherine." Mrs. Fleming takes her umbrella from the stand, opens the front door, and walks into the drizzly day.

Mama carries a basket filled with potatoes, carrots, turnips, and a fresh loaf of bread. She places it by the front door and pulls on her coat.

"Where are you off to, Mama?"

"Remember when we visited Mrs. Merrick? That Welsh woman who lives in the tumble-down hut on Humboldt Street?"

"With three small children?"

"Yes. And it appears she has given birth to another baby boy. How she presumes to feed yet another mouth is a mystery to me." Mama buttons her coat. "We are not so desperate that we cannot help those less fortunate."

"You are always so charitable, Mama."

"Mr. Merrick's family built a fortune, mining Welsh coal pits." She looks in the mirror at the front door as she ties her bonnet. "And now look at them. Financial ruin can happen to anyone, it seems."

In Mama's world, financial ruin is one of the worst catastrophes to befall a family. Perhaps even worse than death. And that fear drives both her melancholy and her compassion.

"Surely you are not going to Kanaka Row on your own. Do you need me to join you?" Humboldt Street, also known as Kanaka Row, after the Hawaiians who came to Victoria for the first gold rush, attracts mostly cutthroats and thieves. Fights and murders are not uncommon in this part of Victoria, and it is not a safe place for respectable women to be alone.

"Mrs. Pemberton is meeting me at the bridge. You stay and help Annie start dinner. I shall be home later."

Annie enters the front foyer and hands Kate a letter. "For you, Miss Kate. From London." Must be from Arthur. Kate waits for Mama to leave, then excitedly rips open the envelope as she runs up the stairs to her room. She wishes his letters could magically appear in the post box the day he writes them, rather than taking months to arrive. She sits at her desk where the light is best.

*London*
*18th Aug '61*

*My dearest Kate,*

*When you write me of the wilds of Vancouver Island—the mountains across the Strait of Juan de Fuca, the surf crashing against the rocky shore, forests of giant coniferous trees, the smell of the damp earth, and open spaces as far as the eye can see—it creates an intense desire in me to one day explore the colony. Did Governor Douglas not call it the "perfect Eden" when he founded his Hudson's Bay fort there? I may be guilty of romanticizing life in the colonies, but you, my dear sister, most definitely sentimentalize what life is like in the big city. Let me absolve you of your notions that London is some kind of paradise.*

*The smells alone would change your mind in an instant. As I've already mentioned to you, the "Great Stink" of '58 was not only disgusting, but the miasma was considered dangerous to human health. The sewage in London has not been ameliorated to any large degree since. Stench is worse in the slums where residents inhale their foul odors down putrid alleys. The stretch of the Thames that is subject to tides brings to low-lying areas raw sewage (since the birth of the water closet), horse and cow dung, refuse from hospitals, chemical works, dye works, fishmongers, slaughterhouse offal, and let us not forget dead rats, birds, dogs, cats, and, sad to say, even dead babies. Do you still wish to live in London, my dear sister? If the answer is yes, in my next letter I will tell you more things to alter your thinking, such as the choking sooty fogs from coal-*

*fired stoves that you can taste in the air, and how the heartbreaking poverty takes its toll on the lower classes who flock from the countryside seeking a livelihood.*

*You continually inquire about my studies at St. George's. The coming term consists of histology (study of the microscopic structure of tissues), osteology, practical physiology, pharmacy laboratory, anatomy, and dissection. Does that satisfy your curiosity? I must tell you something as you are the only one I can truly be honest with, Kate, and I trust you will not breathe a word of this to anyone, especially not to Papa or Mama. I'm living the life of an imposter—I'm not meant to become a physician. You have known my love of art since we were children. Although I had hoped it would, the compulsion to create has not lessened since I began medical school. I have my sketchbook and drawing pencil with me at all times and spend hours in parks, cafes, pubs, even in university classes, sketching whatever or whomever catches my eye. One of our textbooks is* Anatomy: Descriptive and Surgical by Dr. Henry Gray. *(I'm sure Papa has it on the bookshelf in his surgery. Sadly, Gray died in June of smallpox, while attending to his nephew who had the disease.) Instead of being captivated by the scientific details of the human body and the maladies it sustains, I am only taken by the intricate and faithful illustrations of the bones, muscles, organs, and microscopic anatomy by Henry Vandyke Carter. These images have only fueled my desire to recreate the human form on paper or canvas.*

*I know our parents wish me to follow in Papa's footsteps, but I am more cut out for a life in the circus than I am a life in medicine. I am tormented and cannot bear to live the lie much longer. I only wish you were right here to talk sense to me. But, alas ... Please pray for me, Kate.*

*Your loving brother,*

*Arthur*

A ribbon of sunlight shines through the window as Kate holds the letter to her chest. She glances at Arthur's photo on her desk and remembers the last day she saw him. He was only twelve, wearing brown tweed shorts and jacket, with a matching cap, standing on the pier with the school headmaster, waving goodbye to his family as their ship pulled out of the London harbor. His sad expression that day seared into Kate's heart. She is unsure she will ever see Arthur again.

She aches for her brother, who is obviously in agony about living a sham. But she is also angry with him. How could he squander the gift of a superior education and a respectable vocation? She puts the letter in the carved wooden box where she keeps all his letters, and places the box in the bottom drawer of her desk. From her bookshelf she pulls out the few issues of the *Illustrated London News* that moved with them from England. She flips the dog-eared pages to her favorite pictures of life in London—street urchins stealing an apple off a street cart, families picnicking in Hyde Park, the historical Tower of London, and Buckingham Palace. Even the images of factory smokestacks spewing black clouds into the sky fuel her longing.

The sky is blue and clear of clouds, but the breeze is cold and stings Kate's face as she makes her way down Kingston Street. In the tree-felled field at the end of the road, surveyors peer through their instruments that look like giant spiders standing on three long legs. Laborers pound posts into the ground and run strings between the new lots waiting for homes to be built. Kate feels slightly less lonely with the thought of more settlers inhabiting this small town. Onto the wide-open spaces, her memory superimposes her life in London—shops, theaters, chemists, banks, and restaurants line bustling streets; shiny black horses, hooves clip-clopping on the cobblestones, pulling stately carriages; walkways crowded with smartly clothed men and women in the most fashionable dresses, carrying parasols. Her memory fades. All she sees in front of her is emptiness. All she hears are seagulls yelping like puppies and the cold wind singing across the field. She shifts the heavy bag she's carrying from one shoulder to the other, and splashes through the large puddles in her rubber boots, soiling the bottom of her skirt.

A raven circles overhead and then lands on the top of a red alder tree that looks like a skeleton without its summer greenery. The bird peers down, studies her, clucks and squawks. She thinks of Edgar Allan Poe's unsettling poem named after this bird.

> *And the Raven, never flitting, still is sitting, still is sitting ...*
> *And his eyes have all the seeming of a demon's that is dreaming ...*

Kate envies the bird when it takes off from the branch, not tethered to the Earth or to this remote island, as it flaps its wings and soars high into the sky. She reaches the end of Montreal Street and walks along the waterfront. The harbor is almost as busy as her imagined London street. Smoke billows out the stacks of a steamboat heading for the Wharf Street pier. Indian canoes, laden with people and goods, paddle into the harbor to trade or sell their goods in town. A few of Her Majesty's naval ships are at anchor.

She passes the Legislative Buildings, also known as the Birdcages. When the main House of Assembly was built a few years ago, she read an article by the editor of the *British Colonist*, with the impossible name of Amor de Cosmos, who described the building as something between a Dutch toy and a Chinese pagoda. And *The Victoria Gazette* thought the

Legislative Buildings looked like fancy Italian birdcages. She knows next to nothing about architecture, but atop the square building are rooftops that remind Kate of large flat sunhats that Chinese peddlers wear. And the crisscross of detail does resemble an old birdcage she once saw at the market, although it was most likely not from Italy. Through the trees beside the Legislature, Kate sees the Governor's large white house, stately by colonial standards. Kate wonders if Lady Douglas is happily hidden inside, or perhaps she is out delivering a baby.

Kate crosses the bridge over James Bay. Two men wearing soiled and shabby clothes lean against the railing, smoking. She quickens her pace when she feels their scorching stares. These men are most likely part of the wave of new prospectors purchasing their licenses to mine Cariboo gold, whose tents are pitched on the other side of the bay.

Kate remembers three years ago, when tens of thousands of prospectors from all over the world—America, Poland, Italy, France, Germany, and China— arrived on steamers from San Francisco and invaded her small, peaceful town, adding energy and menace, which Kate secretly found exciting. Many prospectors owned nothing more than the cloth-wrapped bundles they carried with them. A sea of gray cotton tents dotted the land from Government Street almost to Spring Ridge, as prospectors camped while purchasing their mining licenses and supplies, in preparation for the trek to the Fraser River Valley. Soon after, all she could hear was the stroke of the chisel and hammer, as shops, saloons, hotels, and wooden shanties were hastily built on every piece of available land surrounding Fort Victoria, the Hudson's Bay Company fur trading post. At the time, Mama would not allow her to walk into town unaccompanied, fearful of the immoral nature and intentions of the miners.

Horses and carriages splash through the water-filled potholes on Government Street as Kate passes the fort, surrounded by its cedar palisade. Men and women pass her on the plank sidewalk, while a group of laborers in dirty coveralls ride beside her in the back of a wagon pulled by reluctant horses.

Kate steps in the door of St. Ann's School on Broad Street and removes her muddy boots. In one classroom, Sister Mary Lumena teaches mathematics to James's class in the Select School—settlers' children whose parents can afford to pay. Across the hall, Sister Mary Conception teaches grammar to the class of Black and Indian children—segregated because colony families refuse to allow their children to mix with other races—and any student whose parents cannot afford to pay for their education. Kate continues to Sister Mary Providence's office at the back of the school, a place of solace for her. Here her curiosity and wonder are always fed an elaborate feast.

She unloads her heavy bag of books on the desk and looks around at the floor-to-ceiling bookshelves that line the room, the map of celestial constellations on the wall, and a wooden crucifix where Jesus hangs dying, head drooped down, ribs sticking out around his concave torso. In the Church of England her family attends, the crosses are bare. Jesus has already ascended to heaven.

On one of the tables, she peers into the shiny brass microscope with the long lens, to see different shaped plant cells that remind her of rocks on the beach. On the floor by the desk, she spins the large world globe held by an ornate teak stand. She finds places that she's read about and imagines—the Buddhist temples in Siam, the tapestries in Persia, the camels and pyramids in Egypt, the Taj Mahal in India, the Amazon Jungle in Brazil. She spins the globe again to find the British Isles, and measures, with her hands spread open, how far London is from Victoria. She then places each returned book on the shelf in alphabetical order. A new book catches her eye: *A System of Natural Philosophy*. She takes it down from the shelf and flips through; words she has never heard before spring off the pages—*hydrostatics ... hydraulics ... pneumatics ... acoustics ... electro-magnetism.*

Sister Mary Providence smiles as she enters her office. "If you are back for more books, I will have to increase my order from England." Her nun's habit is made of layers of heavy black material, with a veil that covers her head and fastens under her chin. One white rim of fabric circles her face. Although her skin is smooth and creamy, her heavy garment makes her look much older than her twenty-four years. Kate doesn't even know the color of Sister Mary's hair.

Kate holds up the book. "May I?"

"I have never met anyone with such an insatiable thirst for knowledge," Sister Mary says in her Irish lilt, as she hangs her cloak on a hook.

"What good does such a thirst do for a woman?" Kate asks. "Singing, drawing, and dancing are the only pursuits women are allowed outside domestic duties."

"Education builds a strong character and a noble heart. Your life will be mostly what you wish it to be."

Kate digests this for a moment. "Did you always wish to become a nun?"

"Even as a young child, I felt a calling to serve. Joining

the Sisters of St. Ann seemed like the best vehicle for this." She walks to the window, where the large silver cross around her neck glints in the sunlight. "My parents nurtured my active mind with the help of governesses and tutors, who taught me poetry, rhetoric, logic, philosophy, mathematics, literature, and history. I was never made to feel ashamed of possessing intellectual talent." She walks across the room, sits, and takes Kate's hands. "God has given you this gift for a reason, Katherine. One day you will find out why."

Can this be true? Kate feels a jolt of possibility pulse through her body.

James appears at the door.

"Did you remember your reader today?" Sister Mary asked.

"Yes, but, Sister, it is far too difficult for me. The words are exceptionally long."

"Exceptionally is a long word and you used it correctly. You are a very clever boy, James. I have every confidence that, if you work hard and practice your reading, it will get easier. You must take your head out of the clouds occasionally."

James nods but he doesn't seem convinced.

Kate packs the book into her bag. Sister Mary hands her another—*A Pictorial History of the New World.*

"You may want this one, as well," she says.

"I am so thankful to you, Sister." Kate adds it to her bag. She feels light, like she could float up into the sky.

James reads from his notebook as they walk across the bridge toward home. "Dup-li-cate, as a verb."

"That means to make or be the exact copy of something."

"What about ... op ... oppressed?"

"That's when people are unjustly or harshly treated. Or constrained, somehow."

"Exasperate."

"That is exactly what you do to me." James looks up at her questioningly and she ruffles his hair. "Come on now, school's over for today."

James puts his notebook into his satchel. "Is Annie really leaving?"

"She and Pete are to be married. Does that make you sad?"

"Not really. When I go to the shops with her, all she wants to do is gossip with her friends who are also housemaids, and she's cross with me when I tell her I want to go home."

"Has Annie not been good to you?"

"I suppose, but she never wants to play with me. And she doesn't know how to read, so she makes up words by looking at the pictures in my storybooks."

"Annie was not hired to play with you, James. She was hired to help care for you, among her many other household tasks."

"May we go to Beacon Hill before home?"

"I need to help Mama and Annie with dinner."

"Please, Kate. I promise I will be a good boy and will not run off and get lost like I did last time." He looks up at her with his big blue pleading eyes.

"Okay, but just for a short time."

"Brilliant!"

"Not too far ahead. Do you hear me?"

James runs down the road past Governor and Lady Douglas's house, heading toward the public park. A great blue heron soars toward the bay.

On the top of Beacon Hill, in a grove of oak trees, James jabs his stick like a musket, pretending to be the Duke of Wellington fighting Napoleon at the Battle of Waterloo. Kate sits in her favorite place, at the base of an old tree, whose large branches spread out like an octopus's tentacles, reading *A System of Natural Philosophy*. She skims the chapters on the pulley, hydraulics, and hydrostatics, but is fascinated by optics and vision. She studies a detailed illustration of the human eye, said to be the most perfect of all optical instruments. It shows the four membranes: the sclerotic, the cornea, the choroid, and the retina, and the two fluids confined within these membranes, called the aqueous and the vitreous humors. Another illustration shows how pencils of light rays flow into the pupil.

> *To render an object visible, therefore, it is only necessary that the eye should collect and concentrate a sufficient number of these rays on the retina, to form its image there, and from this image the sensation of vision is excited.*

Kate's curiosity stirs something inside her, something exciting, but she isn't exactly sure what it is.

"Kate." James points to a naval vessel sailing in the Strait of Juan de Fuca. Ships come and go in Victoria, but this is one of the largest and grandest vessels Kate has ever seen, with its enormous white billowing sails, bow pointing north. Is it heading for the harbor? They watch it move slowly through the water for several minutes, before Kate notices the sun has almost set behind the western hills.

"James, we're late. We must go now." She closes her book and places it into her bag. James throws down his stick and takes Kate's hand as they run down the path toward home.

They arrive at the kitchen door at the back of the house, where Annie and Mama are busy preparing the evening meal.

"Sorry we're late, Mama, we went to Beacon Hill on our way home."

Mama eyes Kate, as she kicks off her rubber boots and puts her book bag on a table.

"I thought perhaps you had one of your long tutorial sessions with Sister Mary Providence," she says, as she carves ham from a shank and places slices on a plate. She makes it clear she doesn't condone Kate's friendship with Sister Mary. Firstly, Mama thinks the Sister is wrong to encourage Kate's scholarship. And secondly, Sister Mary is Catholic.

"We saw the largest ship in the entire Royal Navy coming down the strait," James says. "There were dozens and dozens of gun ports." James takes aim with an imaginary gun, making shooting sounds, pretending he's firing out of one of the ports.

"I overheard Mrs. Kirkham at the market today," Annie says, as she scoops steaming turnips into a bowl. "She said the ship is called the HMS *Forward*."

"*Forward*?" Kate says. "Battleships should be called *Intrepid* or *Destruction* or *Endurance*. Not *Forward*."

"I suppose the name 'Forward' is better than 'Backward' for a battleship," Mama says, smiling.

"The town will be swarming with men in uniform," Annie says.

"Stop your swooning, Annie," Mama says, handing Kate the plate of ham. "It is not becoming. You're soon to be a married woman."

Kate and Annie share a smile, as Kate takes both plates of food to the dining room.

Kate stares at the top of the vegetable bowl that once had much steam rising and now has none. Not a word is spoken at the dining room table. Other than Annie rattling around in the kitchen, the only other sound Kate hears is her growling stomach. Mama sadly stares at the empty chair at the head of the table. Kate can only imagine the chatter going on inside James's head as he fidgets in his chair. As is the case most evenings, Mama, after a painfully long time, finally picks up her fork, which signals dinner will once again begin without Papa.

As Kate puts clean dishes in the antique wooden buffet, she almost drops a plate when she hears Mama singing, something she's rarely heard since they moved to Victoria. When Mama sang to her when Kate was a small child, Kate thought she had the most beautiful voice of anyone in the world— even Jenny Lind, the great opera diva. Kate follows the haunting melody up the stairs to James's room. Mama rests on the bed by a sleeping James, tears streaming down her cheeks, as she caresses his head of brown curls. Kate sits on a chair as Mama sings ...

*While thou, my lover sleep, thy tree its vigil keeps*
*Gently sings the summer where the graceful willow weeps*
*Weeps, oh weeps for thee.*
*Fold my hands and no more grieve me.*
*Love hold me, enfold me*
*In my body, new life mold me.*

When her sad song is over, Mama wipes her tears with a white handkerchief trimmed with delicate lace.

"What is it, Mama?" Kate asks.

"Remember the grand house where we lived near Wimpole Street?" Mama asks. A few more tears streak down her face.

"I do."

"We had a housemaid, a cook, and a coachman."

"Yes, we did. But that was a different time, Mama," Kate says.

"Do you recall the birch and hazelnut trees that surrounded the garden, abounding with honeysuckle, foxglove, and lily-of-the-valley? I would sit for hours while you and Arthur played on the grass, breathing in the floral essence, watching birds and butterflies flitting from flowers to bushes."

Kate remembers that yard well. She and Arthur would play hide-and-seek for hours.

Mama stares out the window at the black night. "I long for those times so profoundly. Every moment of every day I feel my heart may fracture into a thousand pieces."

Kate has never before heard Mama express the depth of her despair, and it scares her.

"I'm sorry you are so desperately unhappy, Mama."

"You were too young to feel the disgrace and shame of losing almost every valuable possession we owned. We were scorned and mocked, not directly to our faces, thankfully, but I could see it in people's expressions, in their eyes." Mama sighs heavily. "When one's wealth and social standing are stripped away, there is very little left."

"But, Mama, surely you don't believe that. We may not

have a grand home with servants and a garden, but we still have each other. Is that not enough?"

"All I wish for, Katherine, is that you will never suffer the same fate as I have."

Mama kisses James's head, picks up a lit candle, and leaves. Mama's recollections elicit Kate's own deep longing for life as it once was. Back then, Kate was convinced Mama's smile, so full of joy, could chase away a storm—when Papa had a thriving medical practice in London, and money was never a concern because their investments were safely in the bank. Arthur lived at home and their family was together.

Kate goes to her bedroom and sits at her desk. Pulls a sheet of paper out of the drawer, dips her pen into the ink, and writes by the light of her fireplace.

*Victoria*

*21 Nov 1861*

*Dearest Arthur,*

*Your letter of 18th August caught me greatly by surprise. You poor soul. Oh, how I wish your letters didn't have to travel by ship across the ocean, taking months to arrive. I can only imagine what has transpired in your life since I last heard from you. You must be in agony, having almost completed yet another university term by now, all the while dreaming a different life for yourself. Or have you even enrolled this term? I have had no word from Mama or Papa that you have written to them. Your next letter will surely tell the story.*

*Putrid sights and smells aside, I long for the bustle of London. Like Mama, I sometimes feel my soul is dying in this wilderness, with not enough to keep it occupied. Sister Mary Providence does her best to keep me in books and intellectual discourse, and I'm forever grateful to her. But I feel stifled, like my corset has been fastened much too tightly and I have no room to breathe. (I apologize if speaking of my undergarments sounds improper, but it is the most apt description I can think of.)*

*Recently I was remembering when Papa and Mama took us to the Great Exhibition. I was just six years old, but I will never forget the palace made of glass, like something out of the Arabian Nights. People from all over the United Kingdom and the world arrived in London by the hundreds. Papa was enthralled with the printing machines and steam engines; Mama, the laces, gloves, silk dresses, rich embroideries, and Queen Victoria's enormous Koh-I-Noor diamond; and you, of course, could not get enough of the French sculptures and paintings. But the boy in you also could not resist the massive penknife with eighty blades. I'm not sure why, but what I remember most are the displays from India, with the enormous stuffed elephant and the animal skins and antlers. Witnessing all the new inventions the world had to offer gave me such hope and optimism, even as a little girl.*

*I wish there were a magic machine that could have us switch places. Why does life only seem to promise such suffering?*

*I long to hear from you again, my dear Arthur.*

*Yours always,*

*K*

# Chapter 4

In the sitting room by the blazing fireplace, Mama stitches tapestry wool into a needlepoint cushion cover, while Kate reads the novel *Vanity Fair* by William Makepeace Thackeray. She takes great care not to provoke Mama by reading any textbooks given to her by Sister Mary—she saves those for the privacy of her room, and keeps them well hidden away under her bed. Although Kate cannot relate to the main character, Becky Sharp, who shamelessly uses her charms to seduce upper-class men, a tug of recognition does nudge her.

> *... until now her loneliness taught her to feign. She had never mingled in the society of women: her father... was a man of talent; his conversation was a thousand times more agreeable to her than the talk of such of her own sex as she now encountered ... the silly*

*chat and scandal of the elder girls, and the frigid correctness of the governesses equally annoyed her.*

Annie knocks on the door and enters. She has a strange look on her face.

"What is it, Annie?" Mama asks.

"Mrs. Fleming is here, Ma'am. And she's brought the native girl."

"Send them in, Annie," Kate says.

"You see ... the girl's father is here, too. They came in the back door and will not leave the kitchen."

Kate and her mama share a look. "Just as well. We will receive them there," Mama says, putting down her skein of wool.

"Here they are," Mrs. Fleming says as Kate and Mama enter the kitchen. "May I present Lucy and her father, Old Pierre." Both Lucy and her father stand close to the door, as if they're ready to escape at a moment's notice. "Old Pierre wanted to meet you and see the house, before allowing his daughter to take the job as housemaid," says Mrs. Fleming. Old Pierre's mouth opens in a toothless grin, and he nods his head. He holds a woven hat the shape of a lampshade.

"I see." Mama smooths down her dress. "He must see that his daughter should be extremely grateful to have employment with a decent family in a well-established household."

Kate has seen native men from various tribes in town—some who wear traditional garb, others who wear clothing similar to White working men. This barefoot man, who smells of campfire smoke, wears only a skirt and a Hudson's Bay blanket over his shoulders that is clipped at the top. His dark skin is creased and his hair matted. At least his daughter's long hair, black as an inkwell, is combed and off her face. Unlike Kate's flyaway curls, her hair is straight as a ruler. Something Kate envies.

"Step forward, Lucy," Mrs. Fleming says. "Let Mrs. Harding have a look at you." Lucy, who looks to be a few years younger than Kate, slowly steps closer and stands in front of her and Mama. Lucy's gaze rests on the floor. Kate is relieved that Lucy is dressed properly in a gray skirt, although Kate thinks her off-white blouse could use a good scrubbing, and the large fake ruby pendant necklace with matching earrings are gaudy and most inappropriate for a housemaid. She observes that this girl's features aren't as harsh as some natives—especially some Nootka, whose skulls are bound at birth with tight bandages to flatten and elongate the head to a narrow point at the crown.

Lucy's long nose sits symmetrically, in the middle of her wide face and above a mouth with full lips.

"Does the girl speak English?" Mama asks Mrs. Fleming.

"Of course. Ask Lucy anything you'd like. She can read and write a little, as well."

"I have been told that you worked as a housemaid before, but I have been a guest at the Gordons," Mama says. "You must know that I have much stricter standards of orderliness and cleanliness. Do you understand?"

Lucy nods, continues to stare at the wooden planks on the floor.

"Always look at me when I speak to you," Mama says. Lucy raises her head and looks directly at Kate's mother with her dark eyes. Does Mama always have to present such an aggressive manner?

"You come recommended by Mrs. Fleming, but I will determine within a short period of time if you have the qualities we are looking for in a housemaid. You may go now and get your things."

Lucy looks nervously at Mrs. Fleming, who nods for her to speak.

"My father wants me home at night. In my village. With my family," Lucy says quietly.

"And why must that be? We prefer a housemaid who will live here under our roof, to look after my young son James during the day when he is not in school, and at all hours of the night, if needed."

Lucy turns and says something to her father in their language. He shakes his head.

"That should be fine, Mama." Kate is embarrassed by her mother's abrupt manner, and doesn't want to chase away their only hope of hiring a housemaid. "As long as Lucy is with us during the day. Besides, James rarely wakes during the night anymore, and if he does, I will tell him to come to me."

"I'm looking for more commitment from our hired help. However ..." Mama scrutinizes Lucy up and down, "if this is all that is available, I suppose we haven't much choice in the matter, now, have we?" She takes a piece of paper off the table and hands it to Lucy. "I had the forethought to obtain a pass for you. You might have to work late into the evenings. I don't want the police calling at our door to say our hired Indian doesn't have her pass to be present in town."

Lucy puts the pass into her coat pocket.

"Our housemaid Annie will show you around the house and explain your duties," Mama says.

Lucy turns and nods at her father. He leaves.

Mama's face is radiant as she watches Papa sitting at the head of the table, carving a roast of beef. The happiest Kate has seen her in weeks. Annie and Lucy bring trays of food to the dinner table. Lucy's hand shakes nervously as she places a plate on the table in front of Kate. She catches Lucy smiling at James before she and Annie leave the dining room.

"Papa, how many bones are there in the human body?" James asks.

"No more questions at the dinner table," Mama says.

"But my son asks a very good question," Papa says, as he places slices of meat onto plates and hands them around.

"William, don't encourage him. Not at the dinner table." She picks up a bowl of vegetables and scoops some onto her plate and hands it to Kate.

"There are two hundred and six bones in our bodies, and over one hundred are found just in our feet and hands," Papa says..

James, wide-eyed, looks closely at his open hands. "But what is the largest bone in our body, Papa?"

"The femur, which is also called the thighbone. It fits into a socket in your hip and connects to your knee."

James stands and looks down his leg.

"Sit down, James," Mama says.

"Do you remember what the bones in the shin are called, James?" Kate asks. She loves this dinner table banter, and wishes Papa could be home every night for dinner.

"I can't remember," James says.

"There are two bones—the tibia and fibula," Kate says.

"Papa, what about—"

"Enough, James, just eat your dinner," Mama says and, teasingly, to her husband,

"You, too."

"What's news from Arthur, Kitty?" Papa says, cutting his meat. "He seems to write to you regularly, but your mama and I have barely heard a word from him lately."

Kate stiffens. "Same interesting full life in England, as far as I can tell." She cuts into her red meat.

"I have a bit of news," Mama says. "Mr. O'Brien is throwing a Christmas ball and has extended invitations to all the officers of HMS *Forward*. Kate, I have ordered you a new gown, especially for the occasion."

"But, Mama, there is no need to buy another gown for me. I have plenty that just gather dust in my closet." The expense of a new gown could pay the housemaid's wages for a month.

"Your grandmama sent some money for just this purpose," Mama says.

"That money should be saved for more important expenses," Kate says.

"The order has been made." Mama folds her arms. "No more discussion."

"But, Papa—"

"I agree with your mama." He puts down his utensils. "You're a beautiful young woman, Kitty, and it's time for you to come out in society."

Coming out in society means that she will be on display for eligible bachelors to examine, as if they were viewing furniture at an auction. The wealthy Mr. O'Brien will surely make the first and highest bid.

In her bedroom after dinner, Kate reads *A Pictorial History of the New World*, on how Northmen, natives of Scandinavia, were the most daring adventurers of Europe, conquering portions of France, England, Germany, and other nations of Northern and Middle Europe. They also visited Greenland and Iceland as early as the ninth century. Before she gets to the chapter on Christopher Columbus, she falls fast asleep, and dreams of sailing far away from Victoria on a Northmen sailing ship.

When she wakes, it's nighttime. How long was she asleep? Out the window, the snow lights up the dark, dismal night. After a long day of work, Lucy walks on the white carpet, leaving a trail of footprints behind her.

"Are you sure you don't want me to show Lucy the shops before I leave?" Annie places her suitcase by the kitchen door and puts on her coat. "Happy to do that for you, Miss Kate."

"On you go, Annie," Kate says. "You've done well, preparing Lucy for her duties. I'll walk with her to town." She hands Annie a wrapped package. "This should keep you warm while you're on the gold trail in the Cariboo." Annie opens the package and pulls out a woolen shawl. "Mama knit it especially for you."

"It's beautiful." Annie opens her small suitcase that carries all her worldly belongings, and there's plenty of room for the shawl. "Would you thank Mrs. Harding for me?"

"Of course. She would have been here to say goodbye herself, but she's at the church, assembling food hampers for parishioners who are sick and elderly."

"Well, I best be going. Pete is waiting for me in town. We must catch a paddle wheeler across the Strait to New Westminster, and we will marry there."

"You're leaving Victoria today?"

"We booked passage on a steamer up the Fraser River to Fort Yale in just two days' time."

"And then what?"

"Then I suppose we follow the wagon trail to the gold fields." Annie pulls on a knitted hat. "Goodbye, Miss Kate."

A deep piercing envy comes over Kate, as if a blunt instrument has been plunged into her stomach and twisted every which way, as she watches Annie skip excitedly away from the house toward her new life.

"We'll first go to the butcher at Queen's Market, where I'll introduce you to Mr. Wilson," Kate says to Lucy, as they trudge through the snow. Near the Birdcages, horses and carriages have stomped down the snow, right across the bridge into town. "He sends us a bill once a month, so you don't have to pay when you pick up the meat." Kate notices that Lucy wears only one earring, the silver tarnished and one of the green stones missing. "Then we'll go to the dry goods store." Lucy pulls her coat collar over her mouth. Kate is sure she must have gotten the coat from the church rummage sale, as it's clearly at least a decade out of fashion. "And at times, we buy produce from the Chinamen who come to our door with their carts, but only if it looks fresh. In town, we prefer the Evan's grocer to the others. The fruits and vegetables are not the finest quality, but they are acceptable and a good price. You will only go to Mrs. Parker's grocery when Mama is having a dinner party. Do you have any questions so far?"

Lucy shakes her head.

They continue to walk in silence, which unnerves Kate. Although their conversations had been limited, she could at least carry on one with Annie.

"Did you enjoy working for the Gordons?"

Lucy nods.

"They were good to you?"

After a painfully long pause, Lucy smiles. "Fish."

"I beg your pardon?"

"Mrs. Gordon liked fish. Salmon. I bring it fresh. Made her very happy."

"Maybe we could get some fish from you, too."

Lucy nods. They walk on.

"You speak English well," Kate says. "When you do speak," she says under her breath.

"I work for English families since I was only eleven."

"How old are you now?" Kate asks.

"Now I fourteen. And I also speak *tenas wawa*."

*Tenas wawa* or Chinook Jargon is the common language of Indians, traders, and missionaries. Papa had to learn this language—a jumbled mix of native languages, English, French, Asian, and Polynesian—since he often visits remote Indian villages.

"Have you attended school?" Kate asks.

"Yes."

"St. Ann's?"

"No, Missionary School."

"Did you enjoy it?"

Lucy hesitates, shakes her head. "Indian children ... not treated well."

Kate doesn't pry but is curious what that means, exactly. Sister Mary has expressed frustration with the Indian students she teaches, many who come and go as they please, and stubbornly choose their own religious views over the ones Sister Mary tries to impart. But she can't imagine any of the sisters mistreating the students.

As they reach the center of town, Kate realizes Lucy is no longer beside her. She turns to see Lucy's face pressed to the window of the jewelry store that recently opened. In the window, beside a pearl necklace and earrings, is a necklace with shimmering turquoise, yellow, and white stones.

"Very beautiful, isn't it?" Kate says. "Those must be real opals."

Lucy is mesmerized.

Kate turns to leave. "We'd best be going before the shops close."

Lucy slowly steps away, but she can't take her eyes off the gems in the storefront.

"Opals," Lucy says. "I could buy those. Pearls, too."

Those gems together would cost hundreds of dollars. Does Lucy know their worth? If so, how on Earth would she have that much money?

As they continue down Wharf Street, a group of mostly young men, in their crisp blue naval uniforms with large gold buttons, walks toward them. Kate knows they must be officers, as the lowly seamen, who have no qualms about whistling and shouting out to her, wear mostly white. By the way the men look around curiously, Kate is sure they must be from the HMS *Forward*. The ship would most likely have set off from either London or Liverpool. Sailing into Victoria Harbour, they must have believed their ship had arrived on a different planet. Kate suddenly feels embarrassed by the provincial town that is her home, and by the admiring looks they give her.

She and Lucy reach a place in the plank sidewalk that has several boards either missing or sticking up, with sharp nails exposed. It would be dangerous to step out onto the road with horses, carriages, and wagons.

"Here, let me assist." One of the uniformed men maneuvers around the hazardous boards and offers his hand to Kate, while his comrades look on, clearly amused. The officer looks at her with pale green eyes and a handsome, friendly smile. His wavy brown hair is tucked under his uniform hat, which is half the height of a top hat. An unfamiliar tingling sensation shoots through her body. Both her face and her body heat up.

"I do appreciate your concern, but we shall be just fine," she says in a more abrupt tone than she would have liked. The other officers elbow each other, laughing. Kate picks up her long coat and steps down into the hole in the walkway, brushes past the green-eyed man, and makes her way around the first broken plank. "Come, Lucy." Lucy reluctantly steps down to the ground. Kate doesn't get very far when the back of her coat snags on a nail.

"Careful or you will rip this beautiful fabric," the man says, crouching down where he can see that she's wearing her old scuffed boots. Did he catch a glimpse of her ankles? He releases her coat from the nail but doesn't let go.

She grabs her coat from him, glances at his smile that is now even wider and showing straight white teeth. Her heart slams against her ribs, as she weaves through the obstacle course of splintered wood with Lucy following. Kate keeps her head down as she steps up onto the plank walkway. Although they stand close enough for her to smell their musky odor, the men part, allowing her and Lucy to walk through. Kate turns for one last look at the handsome officer, but he has been swallowed up in a sea of blue uniforms.

Although it's early evening, the sky is already black. Kate hears James's chatter as she walks up the stairs. She looks into his bedroom, where Lucy is on the floor with him, playing toy soldiers by the roaring fire in the fireplace.

James holds a soldier in front of the one Lucy is holding. "I am the commander here," he says. "You must obey me at all times or it's off to the gallows with you."

"I always obey you, sir," Lucy says.

"I have heard rumors amongst the men. It has been said that you are trying to overthrow the whole regiment."

"I am but a lowly soldier." Lucy bows her soldier.

"And why should I ever believe you?"

"I tell truth."

Kate interrupts. "Time for your bath, James, and then it's off to bed."

"But I bathed last week. Must I bathe again?"

"Yes, you must," Kate says. "Lucy has already heated the water on the stove and will bring it up for you."

Lucy quickly gathers the many soldiers and puts them in a wooden box.

"Race!" James jumps up and does the same. "See how fast I am."

Kate lingers to see the joy on James's face as he cleans up his room. She has not once ever seen a housemaid play with her younger brother. And, for that matter, not once has she played with him.

She reads by the light of the fireplace in her bedroom and tries to concentrate on the structure of the human eye, but her mind is crowded with images of the handsome officer. A warm flood fills her chest, as she replays the meeting over and over again. His pale green eyes ... beautiful smile ... hand reaching out ... her refusing it ... catching her coat on the nail ... releasing her coat from his grip ... chest warm ... body tingling ... thighs pressed together ... walking through the crowd of uniforms ... looking back, but not seeing him.

# Chapter 5

Kate gently removes the bottles from the medicine chest in her father's surgery, while Lucy reads each label as she wipes off the layer of dust with a damp cloth.

"Have you ever needed any of these medicines, Lucy?" Kate asks.

Lucy shakes her head. "My grandmother gives me her medicine."

"Your grandmother?"

"The mother of my father. A healer, collects plants to help sick people." Lucy holds up a bottle of Opium Powder in one hand and Arsenic in the other. "But I have never seen these plants."

"Women can be Indian doctors?" Kate is intrigued.

"Mostly men, but everyone has medicine power."

As Kate wipes down the medicine chest, she wonders why backward natives allow women to be doctors, but her civilized society does not.

"Is your mother also a medicine woman?"

"She died of fever."

"I'm sorry, Lucy." Scarlet fever and measles have taken many lives over the past years, especially among the Indians.

"And her mother died of smallpox many years before her. I never knew that grandmother."

Smallpox. Kate has heard about the devastating disease, but doesn't know much about it.

After the surgery has been cleaned, Kate sends Lucy to put the water on for laundry, as she looks through her father's medical books. She pulls *Anatomy: Descriptive and Surgical* by Henry Gray, off the shelf. Beside it is *A Treatise on the Prevention and Cure of Diseases* by William Buchanan. She hides both books under her apron before she leaves the surgery.

Sitting at her desk in her room, she reads about smallpox in Buchanan's book on disease.

> *The disease, which originally came from Arabia, is now become so general that very few escape it at one time of life or another. It is a most contagious malady; and has for many years proved the scourge of Europe.*

The book goes on to talk about the symptoms: cough, fever, excessive restlessness, difficulty breathing, spots or specks on the eyes, rash and painful blisters that form all over the body. It sounds like the most dangerous and horrible disease imaginable. She then pores over the pages of Gray's anatomy book. Arthur was right—the illustrations of the human form are breathtaking. The layers of muscles, ligaments, and fascia, the intricate network of intertwined veins and arteries, the complex structure of the human skeleton. She's fascinated as she reads about the chemical composition of bone, the structure of the lymphatic glands in the face and in the upper and lower extremities. Nerves and ganglia, the brain and its membranes, organs of digestion. Although she knows it is extremely improper, she also reads about the male organs. She feels a blanket of warmth envelop her face and neck as she studies the illustrations and reads about the workings of the male anatomy. Her face flames when this makes her think of the naval officer.

A knock at her door. She ignores it and keeps reading. Another knock. She closes the book and hides it under her bed. She opens the door to see Lucy on the other side.

"What is it, Lucy?"

"You must come. For tea." Lucy wears Annie's white apron and frilly cap that looks awkward on top of her head, with the long black braid down her back.

"Not now, Lucy."

"Mrs. Harding says."

"Tell her I'm occupied."

"She insists. Mr. O'Brien is here."

"Mr. O'Brien? Again?" Kate says. He has become a more frequent guest lately, dropping in unexpectedly for tea or dinner, and there is no mystery why. He is clearly in the market for a young bride.

Lucy looks concerned, opens the door wider. "Are you well, Miss Kate?"

"Yes, I am quite well."

"What should I tell Mrs. Harding?"

"Tell Mama I will be down shortly." She closes the door and leans her body against it, wishing she could be locked in her room forever with Mr. Gray's anatomy book.

Kate walks into the room. Mama stays seated by the fireplace, while Eamonn O'Brien stands, his open jacket exposing a large round belly. How would she ever share a bed with that massive bulge?

"There she is," he says and bows. He observes Kate so intently from head to toe with his steel gray eyes, it makes her uncomfortable.

She curtseys, briefly holds his outstretched hand. O'Brien sits down.

"Mr. O'Brien and I were just speaking about the Christmas ball he is hosting," Mama says.

O'Brien's gaze follows Lucy when she enters the room, carrying the tea tray. Is the strange look on his face lust or contempt? All Kate knows is it makes her even more ill at ease.

"I have hired musicians all the way from Nanaimo," he says, petting his bushy moustache, as if it were an animal. Kate imagines him kissing her, the wiry hairs prickling her skin. "Is there a song that I could request them to play especially for you, Katherine?"

"I cannot think of one."

Lucy pours the tea.

"Come now, Katherine," Mama says. "You love music." Lucy hands Mama her tea.

"Don't press her, Mrs. Harding." O'Brien unclips a chain from his vest, pulls out a gold pocket watch, swings it from side to side. "As long as I can monopolize Katherine's dance card at the ball, I shall be content." He smiles at Kate as he polishes the watch with a handkerchief. She has only danced at parties with boys her own age that she went to school with at St. Ann's. The thought of dancing with men at the ball suddenly makes her nervous. When Lucy passes him his teacup, O'Brien places the watch on the side table. He puts down the tea and stuffs a biscuit in his mouth.

"Will you buy a license to mine Cariboo gold, Mr. O'Brien?" Mama asks and then takes a sip of tea.

His belly jiggles with laughter, and he almost spews his mouthful of biscuit. "You are very funny, Mrs. Harding." He makes a choking sound, then takes a gulp of tea. Kate and Mama share a look. "Why would I need to mine for more gold when my bank account is already full to overflowing? I am a very astute financier, you see. Whatever I invest in seems to grow my wealth beyond measure."

"Of course," she says, raising her teacup to her lips. Even Mama is getting tired of O'Brien's boastfulness.

As Lucy places another biscuit on O'Brien's plate, she hides the pocket watch under a linen napkin, which makes Kate stifle a laugh. Lucy glances at her as she picks up the empty tray and leaves.

After hearing O'Brien speak about a new hotel he is building, even down to the black swirls in the marble floor,

Kate is greatly relieved when he finally stands to leave. He looks over at the table where he put his pocket watch.

"Where did it go?" he asks.

"What are you missing, Mr. O'Brien?" Kate asks.

"My pocket watch. I left it right here," he says, pointing to the table.

"Are you sure you didn't put it back in your jacket?" Mama asks.

He checks his jacket and vest. "Definitely not." He looks at the door. "Your squaw has stolen it!"

"Look here, Mr. O'Brien," Kate says, uncovering the watch. "You must have placed your napkin over it."

He snaps up the watch. "Still, you need to keep a close eye on your housemaid. Indians may appear to be trustworthy on the surface, but they will steal from you with no hesitation." He stuffs the watch in his jacket pocket, bows, and heads for the door.

*Good riddance, Mr. O'Brien.*

While Kate and Mama peel potatoes in the kitchen, they look out the back window, where Lucy and James are having a snowball fight.

"What nonsense," Mama says. "Your Papa has a patient

in the surgery. All that noise is bound to be disturbing him." She wipes her hands on her apron and starts for the door, but Kate holds her back.

"Mama, they are just playing. If it is noise, as you call it, it is joyful noise. Anyone who is sick or in pain would welcome the sound."

Kate hands Mama the peeler.

"At least Annie knew her place as a housemaid. Did I tell you she sent a note? The grammar and spelling were appalling, mind you."

"What is Annie's news, Mama?"

Mama picks up a potato and begins peeling. "As we predicted, she and her new husband did not make it to the goldfields. Peter has instead joined the crew building the wagon road, while Annie works at a roadhouse, doling out supplies to the miners. What a rough-and-tumble world for such a young girl."

"Annie has a very strong spirit, and I'm sure she will survive very well."

"James will catch his death out there. Look at him. He's already sopping wet."

"Yes, look at him, Mama. See how happy he is. He will dry out and warm himself by the fire."

"Like Mr. O'Brien said, she isn't to be trusted. I have a mind to check her pockets before she leaves every evening."

"Lucy may not know how to cook beef or lamb, and she's not as attentive to cleanliness as Annie, nor does she scrub the laundry as well, but I don't believe she's a thief."

Mama scrapes the potato peels into a pail and takes another long look out the window.

"On the subject of Mr. O'Brien, from all appearances, he will soon propose to you."

"He will be disappointed if he's expecting a dowry."

"I am sure he's well aware of our meagre circumstances."

"And it is my role as daughter to marry into wealth, to pull the Harding family out of our debt?"

Mama is taken aback by Kate's forthrightness.

"I'm too peculiar, Mama," Kate says. "I will always love my solitude more than I will love any man."

Mama laughs softly. "Oh, my darling, where do you get these notions? Love is not a necessary ingredient for marriage."

"Did you not love Papa when you married?"

"Our families made a good match. I liked him well enough. One can only hope that fondness grows."

"Fondness? But that is not enough for me, Mama."

"Do you really believe that you have any choice in this

matter?" Mama says in a calm voice. "Go to your father. Tell him dinner will be ready shortly."

Kate leaves the kitchen. If she married Mr. O'Brien, would her fondness for him grow? Something deep inside tells her it wouldn't. What about the handsome officer? Would he be a man she might love? When she gets to the front hallway, she stares at the door. Seized by the realization of how trapped she feels in her life, she grabs her coat off the hook and pulls it on. She grasps the door handle. Her breath is fast and heavy. She could do it. She could just leave. Run as far away from here as she can. Stow away on a ship that's sailing for the Orient. She holds the cool brass for several moments, then sinks to her knees, her coat and dress swelling out around her. Like a trapped animal in a very small cage.

After several minutes, Kate stands, hangs her coat back on the hook, and slowly walks down the hallway to the back of the house. She waits outside the open door of the surgery, as Papa hands a bottle of tonic to a gray-haired woman with a humped back. Papa works so hard, gives so much of himself to the residents of this town. Mama is resentful of the time he devotes to his patients, but it makes Kate proud.

"Take this when needed, Mrs. Thorton. If your problem persists, increase the dosage. I've written it all out for you."

"Thank you, Dr. Harding." She takes her medicine and shuffles out the door.

Kate looks at the bottles on the shelf. "What was the medicine you prescribed for Mrs. Thorton, Papa?"

"That is confidential between a doctor and his patient."

"You know you can trust me. I would never tell a soul."

Papa looks at her for a long moment. "Sulfur."

"And how will sulfur help her?"

Papa begins sorting the files on his desk. "It's a laxative, acts on the large intestines, also relieves hemorrhoids and irritable bowels. I also prescribe it for chronic coughs, which old coachmen seem to be troubled with."

"And why are old coachmen prone to chronic coughs?"

Her papa laughs. "I do admire that curious mind of yours, but you must stop."

"Tell me, Papa. Please."

"Coachmen work outside their whole lives in all kinds of weather, not to mention tending to the horses. They are bound to contract a chronic respiratory condition."

Kate goes to the bookshelf and pulls out her papa's notebook, *Diseases, Treatments, and Medicine.* "May I borrow this, just for tonight? I promise I will return it first thing in the morning."

"You know your mama would not wish me to encourage you."

"She does not have to know. Besides, if I don't study new things, my curious mind, as you call it, will wither and die. You wouldn't want that on your conscience, would you? Please, Papa?"

"But to what end, Kitty?"

She has no answer for him. All she can do is shrug and shake her head.

He looks at her for several moments. "My dear, how I wish life could be different for you." He slides a stack of papers into a folder. "You can take it, but just for tonight. If your mama finds out, you will tell her you removed it from the surgery without my knowledge."

"Thank you." Kate kisses his cheek. "Dinner will be ready soon." She hides the contraband under her apron and leaves the surgery.

Kate and her parents sit at the long dining room table, as Lucy brings a plate of potatoes and carrots, and places a platter with steaming baked salmon in front of Papa.

"What a delicious looking fish," he says as he carves out portions.

"Lucy brought the salmon fresh this morning from the reserve," Kate says as Lucy exits the dining room.

"And she taught us how to bake it much like the natives do," Mama says, and even looks pleased.

"Well, well." Papa begins filling his plate. "Did James partake of this delightful feast?"

"He ate in the nursery with Lucy," Kate says.

"He seems to be getting very much attached to her," Papa says.

"Against my better judgement." Mama scoops vegetables onto her plate.

"Is it not good that James adores our new housemaid, Mama?"

"Of course, I'm pleased to see James so content in Lucy's care. But I have heard that Indian servants often leave without notice," Mama says, flaking off a forkful of salmon.

"We don't know that will happen for sure, Louisa," Papa says.

"It just worries me that in addition to finding a new housemaid in this impossible place, we'll have a grieving boy to contend with as well," Mama says. Kate notices her voice is softer, less severe.

Kate eavesdrops outside James's bedroom door, open a crack.

"Sun is father," Lucy says. "He speaks for us."

"You are quite wrong, Lucy," James says. "I have never heard the sun speak. Not one word. It has no voice. It is a fiery ball of gas that sits high up in the sky and shines down on us each day."

James needs a talking to about being cheeky to their housemaid.

"Learn to hear your spirit, little man. Sun watches you at all times. Listens while you pray."

If Mama knew Lucy was telling James Indian stories, she would be let go faster than a blink. But how is a sun that speaks any more fanciful than the parting of the Red Sea, or a man surviving in the belly of a whale for three days? She peeks into the room.

"I am supposed to pray to the Lord Jesus every night." James kneels by his bed and presses his hands together.

"Only one god." Lucy shakes her head. "How can that be believed?"

He presses his hands together and recites the prayer: *"Now I lay me down to sleep, I pray thee Lord my soul to keep. If I die before I wake, I pray thee Lord my soul to take. If I live another day, I pray thee Lord to guide my ways."*

James looks up at Lucy with a crinkled brow. "I hope Jesus does not take my soul tonight."

Lucy pulls back the heavy gray bedspread with geometric patterns and lifts James back onto the bed." I will not let your Jesus take you away. Ever."

"What do you think happens after we die, Lucy?"

"We are reborn again and again. Your soul carried from one life to the next. It travels to the home of *Skwinonet,* animal spirits like the sky, the woods, or the ocean, before coming back to Earth."

Kate peeks down the hall to make sure Mama is nowhere near.

"I would like my soul to visit the ocean and swim with the killer whales." James moves his hand up and down like the waves.

"The whale may become sea wolf and visit your dream tonight." Lucy pulls back the bedspread.

"I do hope so," James says as he crawls under the covers. "I would so love to dream about a sea wolf."

Kate imagines James coming into her room later with a nightmare about a sea wolf spirit.

Kate goes to her room, closes the door, and jams a chair up against the handle. She kneels down, reaches under her bed, and takes out Papa's notebook. The anatomy book, which she was supposed to put back on Papa's shelf, is also still there. She opens her desk drawer, reaches under a stack of paper, and pulls out a new notebook. She fans the blank pages and breathes in the smell that reminds her of toasted nuts. Kate dips her pen in the inkwell and starts a record of her father's medical findings.

***Diseases, Treatments, and Medicine by Dr. William Alfred Harding***

*Digitalis Purpurea—a sedative poison and diuretic. Its sedative affect calms a fluttering heart. In small doses, pulse slower, relieves constipation and troublesome head pain ... no true antidote known for poisonous doses of Digitalis.*

*Arsenic—for the treatment of fever... in chronic diseases of the skin, such as yaws ... a danger of its absorption ... if eyelids become stiff its use must be stopped. Also treatment for syphilis and chronic Rheumatism.*

*Zinc—prevents respiratory ailments and infections of the ear ... the sulfate employs a tonic effect on the nervous fibrilla ... an excellent emetic which produces little nausea and acts very quickly. Treatment for Epilepsy, the most intractable disease ... there is no organic mischief.*

The night is black and still. The candle is almost burned right down, as Kate continues to pore over her father's notes. A knock on her door. She quickly stuffs Papa's papers in her desk and pushes the textbook under her bed.

"Who is it?" she asks through the door.

"Lucy."

Kate takes the chair from under the handle and opens the door.

Lucy's forehead is creased with worried lines. "I saw the light in your window."

"Why are you still here? It's awfully late."

"My canoe. Gone."

"What canoe?"

"To paddle across water. To my village."

Of course, Lucy would need a boat to cross the harbor each day to and from the Indian reserve. It suddenly dawns on Kate that Lucy navigates her way home in the pitch dark each night, with only the moon and stars to light her way. She pictures herself on the water, high winds tossing the boat, the pounding rain and icy air chilling her to the bone. Lucy's vulnerable expression belies a courage Kate could never imagine herself possessing.

"You can sleep in Annie's old room. You'll find sheets and blankets in the cabinet, and a nightgown in the dresser."

Lucy starts down the dark hallway.

"Wait." Kate lights another candle, places it in a holder, and hands it to Lucy. Her footsteps creak on the wooden floor, as she makes her way down the hall to the housemaid's room.

In the faint flickering light of her candlewax puddle, Kate looks in the mirror, as she takes out the pins holding up her hair and lets it fall down her shoulders and back. As she undresses, she beats down her shame and imagines the Navy officer slowly unbuttoning her blouse, feels the fabric brush her skin.

She blows out what remains of her candle, puts another log in the fireplace, and crawls under her thick bedspread. Soon she falls asleep.

*Rocking in a hollowed-out shell of wood. Grasping. Swaying. Stomach churning. Rain buckets down. Waves crashing. Desperately alone. Ocean. Surrounded by ocean. Haunting loon's call. Sound of death? Where is it? Rain. Clothing glued. Hair clings. Shivering. Water overflowing canoe. Frantic. Loon calls again. Wooden bones swallowed. Gasping. Thrashing. Relentless waves. Choking. Body sinks. Down. Down. Green silk hovers. Black hair drifts. Down. Deeper. The loon. Its gray head. Feathers like black and white checks. Circles around. And around. Red eye stares.*

Kate shoots up in bed, her body shaking. Soaked in sweat, hair pasted to her head.

# Chapter 6

After a restless night and terrifying dream, Kate feels unsteady as she walks down the stairs. Mama waits for her at the bottom.

"Mama, what is it?"

"That man is here again."

"Mr. O'Brien?"

"Of course not, Katherine. Lucy's father."

"He must be here to see if Lucy is well. Her canoe went missing last night and she had to sleep in the housemaid's room."

"I wondered how she got such an early start this morning," Mama says.

Kate and Mama enter the kitchen, where Lucy talks quietly with Old Pierre at the back door. He has the same wild hair and wears the same skirt and Hudson's Bay blanket around his shoulders. But today he wears old ragged army boots. He nods and grins at Kate and her mother. Both nod back. After a few more words with Lucy, Old Pierre leaves down the path toward the barn.

"My canoe was floating in the harbor." Lucy cracks eggs into a bowl and whisks them. "The wind sent it there."

"Poor man. He must have been worried sick that you had drowned," Mama says.

Kate's vivid dream suddenly blazes through her mind. Choking on the salty ocean water. Waves slapping her under. Sinking. Giving up, until ... the loon. Circling and circling with its penetrating ruby-red eyes. She tries to shake the disturbing dream out of her mind.

As Kate and Lucy step out of the market with sacks of fresh vegetables, they sidestep to avoid the splatter of slushy snow from horses' hooves and wagon wheels. On Wharf Street, Kate hears the clanking of chains and the shouts of crewmen working on the ships at anchor in the harbor. The smell of coal infuses the air. A few brave men race up flimsy ropes by the masts that reach up to the sky. She read in *The British Colonist* that naval vessels are at anchor in Esquimalt Harbour, but she is unsure if the HMS *Forward* is one of them.

When the sky clears, it seems the whole town swarms out of their homes onto downtown streets, like dressed-up rodents poking their noses out of their winter homes. Ladies gossip outside the shops; children chase dogs or each other; and gentlemen look right through Lucy but tip their top hats to Kate.

"Mama does not like me going near the Johnston Street Ravine, but Papa's shirts must be picked up from the Chinese tailor. As our housemaid, you are not to be seen anywhere near this area without Mama or myself. Do you understand?"

Lucy nods.

"And under no circumstances are you to be here at night, even with your pass."

As they walk by the horse stables and livestock pens, Kate covers her nose to mask the odor. London isn't the only city with putrid smells—even Victoria has foul-smelling drains and ditches. They turn down Fisgard Street. The dwellings in Chinatown are rundown, with shacks made of thin tilting boards, crammed one beside another. But Kate feels safer here than in seedy places such as Kanaka Row or some areas of Fort Street. Languid men in silk jackets, with long black braids hanging down their backs, sit on the walkway or at small tables, playing games they brought from China. They glance at Kate but don't leer like other men. Could it be the opium that has more of a calming influence, compared to alcohol's perilous force?

A bell clangs as they enter the tiny tailor shop. It smells of dust and stale smoke, with boxes and bolts of fabric—all for men's suits and shirts— piled by the small glass counter. The clinking sound of a sewing machine stops, and a man flips open a red brocade curtain with gold tassels that closes off the back room. He wears a smartly fitted navy-blue plaid suit and a white dress shirt with a bright orange neck scarf. Mama refuses to patronize the other Chinese tailors, who wear traditional costumes. She thinks it most inappropriate, especially for a tailor who should be showing off his skills.

"Good day, Mr. Cheung. Shirts for Dr. Harding, please."

He peers behind Kate and scowls at Lucy. Shouts something in Chinese and makes a gesture as if he's shooing out a pesky dog.

"She is with me. Lucy is our new housemaid."

His voice is louder and his gestures more frantic.

"I beg your pardon, sir ..." His behavior angers Kate.

"I wait outside," Lucy says as she turns to leave.

Kate exits the shop with the shirts wrapped in brown paper. "Mr. Cheung was extremely rude to you."

Lucy takes the packages from her. “He treat me no different than most.”

The resigned look on Lucy’s face engulfs Kate with shame. She knows that, in the past, she would have accepted Mr. Cheung’s and even Mama’s behavior. She would even have thought it fitting. Who would ever want an Indian in their shop or home? She was taught to believe the English have moral superiority over the Chinese, as well as the Indians.

On Fort Street, they pass hotels and saloons, where down-and-out men of every skin color loiter at the entrances, smoking cigarettes. Their piercing stares send a creepy shiver up Kate’s back. These destitute men must be some of the hundreds of miners who never struck gold in the Fraser Valley. A few blocks further, the road is lined with shanties that Kate knows are brothels. Many are filled with Indian women who are slaves, forced into prostitution by their native captors. She read in *The British Colonist* that these establishments have been recently licensed as “dance halls.” This angered the editor, Amor de Cosmos, who called them “sinks of iniquity and pollution.” Kate wonders if these sinks of iniquity are what keeps the miners occupied in their own enclave, and mostly separated from civilized society.

She cranes her neck to scan the navy officers in their blue uniforms, strolling on the other side of the road.

"He is not among them," says Lucy, smiling.

"I have no idea what you're talking about." Kate looks straight ahead, feels her cheeks turn warm, knowing she's not fooling anyone—not Lucy, not herself. Wonders if her handsome officer would visit this heinous part of town.

Two Indian women spill out from one of the brothels onto Fort Street in a brawl. With bodies swaying to keep upright, they pull hair, punch, and kick one another. Kate is disgusted when a group of White, Indian, and Chinese men look on amused, some shouting and clapping, encouraging the fight. She wishes she were brave enough to tell the men that they are the root cause of these women's misfortunes. As she has discussed with Mrs. Fleming, if the men were not willing to pay for the service, perhaps these women would find another means of making a living.

Lucy calls out something in her own language. The woman with a bloody nose glances at Lucy, but continues pounding the other woman with her fists.

"Do you know that woman?" Kate asks.

A native man, who obviously runs the establishment, hurries out of the brothel and approaches the brawling women.

He struggles to pry them apart, grabbing the woman Lucy spoke to. When she takes a swing at him, he slaps her face, tries to drag her by the arm back to the brothel. Lucy storms up to him, pulls a knife out of her coat pocket, and holds it to his throat. The steely look on her face frightens Kate.

"Lucy, no!" Kate says, totally shocked at what she's witnessing.

The man lets go of the woman, holds his hands up in surrender, and slowly backs away. Lucy sheathes her knife and tucks it away. The woman tries to fight her, yells as Lucy ducks a punch. After more cursing and flailing, the woman finally allows Lucy to talk her into going back inside.

Lucy joins Kate and they walk in silence. Kate doesn't even know where to begin to ask what just happened.

"My aunty," Lucy says. "The drink stole her spirit."

Kate looks over at Lucy's aunt staggering back to the brothel, yelling at no one. Victoria has never been the same since liquor flowed in on the first tidal wave of the gold rush. There are now more drinking establishments and liquor outlets than grocery stores, which has caused much debate among the citizens. Kate has witnessed the devastating effect of liquor on Indians and Whites alike, but Papa says alcohol has an exaggerated influence on the Indians. What is it about their physical constitution that make this so? Is it something in their blood? Maybe she'll find the answer in one of her textbooks.

Outside St. Ann's school, Kate hands Lucy a sack of vegetables.

"I'll walk James home when school is finished. You go back and start preparing dinner. Remember not to stew the mutton too long. The last time you cooked it, the meat tasted like shoe leather." By the hurt look on Lucy's face, she wishes she could take back her brusque tone.

Lucy shuffles the bags in her arms and starts down the road.

"Did you know, Sister, that the Songish allow women to be Indian doctors?" In a storage room, Kate helps Sister Mary unpack boxes of new textbooks. "And here we English view natives as an inferior race of people."

"Is it medical studies that interest you, Katherine?"

"Perhaps I'm making up for my brother's lack of interest, but lately I seem to be gobbling up everything I can about medicine and the human body. My father's medical texts and papers fascinate me." Kate takes an armful of books out of a box. "How all the complex organs and systems work in harmony, and what medicines or treatments the body needs when it breaks or is diseased. *The System of Natural Philosophy*, the book you lent me, even illustrates the intricate workings of the human eye."

"Is this a passion you wish to pursue?" Sister Mary places textbooks on an empty shelf.

"If it were somehow available to me, then yes, of course. But it's not, and I can't imagine it ever will be."

"Would it surprise you that I know of a woman who studied medicine?"

Kate is shocked. "But surely no university in the world would admit a female student."

"That is not true. My cousin Daniel immigrated to America to attend Geneva Medical College in the state of New York. A woman named Elizabeth Blackwell graduated just a few years before he did—top student in her class."

"Why is this not common knowledge?" Kate is too intrigued to continue unpacking books.

"Assuming the all-male student body would never agree to a woman joining their ranks, the faculty allowed them to vote on her admission. As a practical joke, they voted yes, and her admission was accepted, even though both students and faculty had serious misgivings."

"Have any other women graduated from that medical school?"

"Blackwell was ostracized, not only by the professors and her fellow students, but also by the patients she was meant to train with. Because of her many challenges, I'm not sure any other woman has attempted to follow in her footsteps."

"Where is she now?"

"Daniel heard that she studied in medical clinics in London and Paris, before she set up the New York Infirmary for Poor Women and Children."

Women as doctors. Could this be? How could she possibly pursue this? University is expensive. Where would the money come from? What would Papa say? Mama would never support it, even if the family weren't burdened by financial troubles. She forces herself to hold onto a glimmer of hope.

Kate quietly closes the front door behind her, hangs her coat on the rack. She hears the clinking of pots and pans from the kitchen, while Mama gives directions to Lucy. She hears them both laugh, which comes as a big surprise to Kate. Now that Mama is getting to know Lucy, she seems to be finally warming to her.

The stairs creak as Kate tiptoes up to her room.

*15 Dec 1861*

*My dearest Arthur,*

*My head feels detached from my body, as if it is floating in the clouds. I look around at all that should be familiar, but everything appears strange and distorted, like when I was a child looking through Grandmama's eyeglasses.*

*Sister Mary told me today that over a decade ago, a woman—an Elizabeth Blackwell—graduated from a medical school in the state of New York. Remember when I wrote you, fantasizing about a machine that could magically have us switch places? My soul starves for that device now more than ever. There you are, shackled to a career you have no desire to pursue, and here I am, craving to study medicine with every cell in my body. Yes, it is true, dear brother, I have been devouring Mr. Gray's* Anatomy: Descriptive and Surgical, *praying that Papa doesn't miss it. And I've also been transcribing Papa's notes on healing medicines and tonics into my own reference book. The other night Papa asked me to what end am I devoting so much time to this scholarship. Of course, I had no answer for him. But with this new knowledge today from Sister Mary, perhaps there is a reason. And now only you know the depth of my passion for medical studies and that it may be what keeps me alive.*

*Will either of us have the courage to break out of our respective molds, strong as steel, that crush our spirits? Perhaps if one of us makes the attempt, that bravery will inspire the other.*

*I long to hear how you are managing, my dear Arthur. I will patiently await your next letter.*

*Yours forever and always,*

*K*

# Chapter 7

Kate stands in front of the large oval mirror while Lucy cinches the last of the fasteners on the back of her corset. The thought of seeing the handsome naval officer at the ball crowds her thoughts. She hopes Mr. O'Brien does not fill her entire dance card, and there will be at least one dance available for the officer. Or will he favor some of the other eligible young women in Victoria, like Fanny or Emily? Although ashamed to even think it, Kate knows she has an advantage over the others in terms of appearance—even complete strangers have commented on her beauty since she was a little girl. But what good is possessing beauty when it is only a commodity to be sold off to the highest bidder? Aside from Papa, men seem only to want a pretty possession that keeps silent most of the time.

She turns her head to admire her hair that Mama coiffed in a magnificent nest of curls, knots, and braids. And the pastes and powders Mama applied to her face and décolletage, the different shades of paint on her eyelids, cheeks, and lips, have added vibrancy to her pale complexion. She steps into the hoop cage that gives shape to her flowing bell-shaped skirt and ties it. Lucy brings her the gown that was laid out on the bed and slips it over her head. White silk taffeta dotted with delicate cobalt blue embroidered flowers, and more than enough fabric for the skirt to hide the lines of the hoops. The bodice fits perfectly and sits nicely off her shoulders. Although her frame is thin, she has full round breasts and feels her cleavage is too much on display with the low, rounded neckline. Kate has to admit this gown Mama had custom-made in San Francisco is gorgeous, although it looks much too similar to a wedding gown for her liking. She presumes Mama planned it that way.

"How do I look, Lucy?"

What a vain question. She has probably never looked this pretty in her entire life, but part of her is truly curious what Lucy thinks. "Beauty is in the eye of the beholder," and what is deemed beautiful varies among the races.

Lucy glances in the mirror. "Like a dancer spinning in a jewelry box."

"Where did you see such a box?"

"Church market. It played music."

"Did you buy it?"

"Not enough dollars then. But I have riches now."

How much money could Lucy have? She gets paid very little as a housemaid.

Kate takes a necklace off her dresser and hands it to Lucy. She puts on the matching earrings. Lucy's eyes widen with fascination as she studies the teardrop lapis stones as if they were dug up from a treasure chest. "This ... this is beautiful."

"It's Mama's. From Paris." She wonders if Lucy knows where Paris is.

Lucy gently rubs her thumb on the largest stone, and carefully inspects the other gems.

"You do appreciate beautiful jewelry, Lucy." Although the silver dangling earrings Lucy wears are dull and tarnished.

"I will marry well."

"How so?"

"More earrings, bracelets, and necklaces, the better match I will make."

A collection of old jewelry is to be Lucy's dowry?

After several admiring moments, Lucy finally places the chain of gems around Kate's neck and clasps it. Kate takes one last look in the mirror. The glamorized bait for Mr. O'Brien's marriage trap.

The coachman assists Kate up the steps of the covered carriage Mr. O'Brien has sent for them. Inside, the smell of stale cigars and whiskey irritates her nostrils. Except for the ceiling, the carriage is entirely covered in gaudy royal blue jacquard—she's not at all surprised by Mr. O'Brien's garish taste. Before she sits on the plush padded seat, Mama arranges the mounds of fabric of Kate's gown under her overcoat so it won't crease.

"Walk on," the coachman commands the horses, as the carriage lurches forward down the drive.

"What a gentleman Mr. O'Brien is," Mama says. "Sending us such luxurious transport."

"Nora and our small carriage would have gotten us there just the same," Kate says.

Papa cracks a smile but quickly wipes it off his face.

"Such nonsense." Mama, her mouth in an anxious line, is most likely playing over in her mind the different scenarios of how Kate will embarrass her by rebuffing Mr. O'Brien's attention. Kate is surprised Mama even decided to come to the ball, since she's still in mourning. She does look striking, even in black woolen moiré.

"You look beautiful this evening, Kitty," Papa says with

a proud smile. “I may have to single-handedly fight off all your suitors.”

“And you look especially dashing tonight, Papa.” He wears a bow tie, crisp white shirt (which she taught Lucy how to iron), his black evening jacket, and top hat.

“Why, thank you, my dear.” He tips his hat.

“William, please be mindful that Katherine has only one suitor this evening.”

Papa gives Kate a sympathetic look.

Everyone in Victoria knows a marriage proposal from O’Brien will be imminent the day after her seventeenth birthday, in less than five months’ time. Everyone except for the navy officer with the pale-green eyes. Although gossip in Victoria travels as fast as a steam engine, so even he may have heard. Much to Mama’s dismay, it was Papa who insisted that Kate be seventeen years of age before he would allow a formal proposal.

She pulls back the gold curtain and peers out into the clear night, trying to calm herself, looking up at the partial moon that dimly lights the sky. The thrumming of drums from the Songish reserve across the water keeps time with her heartbeat.

Guests dressed in their finest attire exit carriages lined up in front of Ballymoon Manor, named after a castle in

Ireland. When their carriage finally pulls up to the front door, the coachman offers his hand to help Mama and Kate as they step out. The manor is as tall as the Windsor Hotel, with two white pillars that offset the sand-colored exterior stonework. Kate lifts the heavy material of her skirt, as she makes her way up the long stairs to the front entrance. O'Brien, wearing a bright green velvet vest under his black evening suit, stands at the top of the stairs, greeting his guests. His long forehead is shiny in the light of the lamp, and his usually bushy hair is greased down.

"The Harding clan has finally arrived," O'Brien says when they reach the top of the stairway. "I have been waiting patiently."

"Eamonn, it's a pleasure to be here," Papa says, and shakes hands.

"It is my pleasure, I assure you." He turns to Mama. "Mrs. Harding, you look especially lovely this evening." He gives her outstretched hand a quick peck.

"Thank you, Mr. O'Brien," Mama says and curtseys.

Kate feels his probing eyes on her. She looks down at her dress that has spread out around her. "My dear, Katherine. Your beauty takes my breath away." And the smell of whiskey and tobacco on his breath takes hers away.

"Thank you for your kind words, Mr. O'Brien," Kate says and curtseys. She senses his gaze travel up and down her body, and squirms when he plants his lips and scratchy moustache on her hand. His wet mouth stays on her hand for an uncomfortably long period of time. Why have her feelings for Mr. O'Brien changed so drastically in such a short while? She was never greatly attracted to him but found him a fairly charming and pleasant man. Why does she now feel repulsed around him? It must have something to do with meeting the handsome officer that she cannot clear out of her mind.

"I hope you don't mind, but I have taken the liberty of filling in my favorite dances on your card." He hands Kate the little booklet bound with gold ribbon. "Only four, mind you. I don't want to deprive you of dancing with other gentlemen. And there will be many others lining up, I assure you."

"Very kind of you," Kate says. Mama smiles as Kate takes the dance card from Mr. O'Brien and slips her hand in the looped gold ribbon. Perhaps there will be a dance for the officer after all. They go inside.

Three maids greet them in the large wood-paneled foyer and take their coats. Lively orchestra music can be heard coming from the ballroom. Festive green and red ribbons hang from the walls, and an enormous decorated Christmas tree stands at the back. Although it's only four days until Christmas, this is the first time Kate has felt the spirit of the season. Other maids scurry around, taking coats from guests. Where did O'Brien find all this hired help? Perhaps as he did with the orchestra, he had his maids brought in from outside of Victoria just for the ball.

In the dining room, buffet tables are filled with platters of meat, fish, and vegetables, as well as pyramids of exotic fruits. Kate follows her parents into the ballroom. They stop to converse with members of Victoria's elite—including the Helmckens and Governor Douglas (of course, Lady Douglas is absent). Emily and Fanny dance the polka with Henry and Philip, boys who also graduated with her from St. Ann's. She scans the dancers as well as those watching on the side, but she doesn't see even one blue uniform. Perhaps HMS *Forward* was called back out to sea. Polarized feelings of disappointment and relief wash over her all at once. Disappointment at the prospect of not meeting the officer, and relief that she won't be O'Brien's prize, on display for him to witness.

The ballroom is tastefully decorated. Delicately carved cornices trim the corners of the ceiling; valances made of exquisite sheer fabric sweep over large windows; and chandeliers twinkle as the light catches the countless dangling crystals. The cost of keeping all those oil lamps lit for an evening would pay Papa's salary for a week, maybe longer. Could she ever conceive of being the lady of this exquisite manor? Her family would never again have to worry about money. Arthur could pursue his artistic passion in Paris, or any other city in the world, for that matter. James could go to the finest boarding school and the most prestigious university in England. This life would easily afford fancy dinners and parties and balls ... fine food shipped in from Europe, America, and the Orient ... dresses designed and tailored in the latest styles in Paris ... trips to New York and London ... cooks and maids ... carriages and coachmen. Her lot in life is to sacrifice her own dreams—her purpose, as Sister Mary calls it—for her family's financial wellbeing.

When the dance is over, Fanny, Emily, and the young men make their way over to where she's standing. Philip, tall and thin as a reed, sports a scruffy moustache that is trimmed shorter on one side. His trousers are about two inches too short. A typical colonial boy. Henry is not particularly tall but has broad shoulders and a face that's not quite handsome, yet open and friendly. He and Kate vied for top marks at school. The difference is that his intellect has afforded him the opportunity to study history at Oxford University next fall, whereas Kate will most likely go nowhere. She knows neither boy well, since the social gatherings among her peers usually involve silly games, and even sillier conversation, that she cannot abide.

"My goodness, Kate, you look stunning," Fanny says. By the expression on their faces, it's clear both Philip and Henry concur.

"You two, as well," Kate says. In fact, the fabric of Fanny's gown resembles the color of seaweed, but it is definitely more tasteful than Emily's that looks to be made of drab drapery fabric, with her doughy breasts bulging through a lacy fabric on the neckline. When did she become so judgmental about appearances? And so vain about her own looks.

"Isn't this just a splendid ball?" Emily says, looking around. "I haven't been to one this grand since Governor Douglas hosted the New Year's Ball last year."

"Yes, it's grand, indeed," Kate says with as much warmth and enthusiasm as she can muster.

"You must fill a plate in the dining room, Kate," Emily says. "The asparagus and sautéed mushrooms are splendid, and the duck and veal will melt in your mouth." She licks her lips.

"When I am hungry, I will do just that."

"Mr. O'Brien must surely have brought in a French chef for the occasion," says Fanny.

"Oh, that must be Rebecca Thompson," Emily says, pointing to a young woman chatting and laughing with Mr. Connelly, a banker and one of the eligible bachelors in town. "She's Mrs. Bennet's niece, who just arrived from New York City. I heard she won't be leaving to go back to America until June." Rebecca has golden hair and wears a beautiful silk gown the color of sage, with matching jewel-covered ribbons flowing down the skirt. Her smile is open and warm. She is striking. An icy feeling slithers into the pit of Kate's stomach. Is this unpleasant feeling because she is no longer the prettiest girl in the room? Is she really that shallow? She pinches her hand to admonish herself.

"May I?" Philip asks, pointing to Kate's dance card. When she hands it to him, he flips the pages. "Mr. O'Brien didn't leave much room for the rest of us, now, did he?"

Kate flushes as Philip writes his name down and hands the dance card to Henry's outstretched hand.

The music and dancing come to a stop, couples rearrange themselves on the dance floor and wait for the orchestra to start up. "It looks like our dance is up next, Kate," Henry says. "A Quadrille."

"Shall we, then?" Kate rests her hand on Henry's as they walk to the dance floor to join three other couples to form a square for the Quadrille. When the music begins, Kate curtseys to Henry and then to the man on her other side. After she dances several steps with the man across from her, Henry twirls her and she catches a swath of blue from the corner of her eye. When it's her turn to chasse across to her partner, she faces the group of navy officers mingling with the other guests. She moves left when she should have gone right, distracted, checking to see if the handsome one is among them. As far as she can tell, he isn't.

After a polka with Mr. O'Brien, which Mama happily watches, clapping in time to the music, and a redowa with Philip, his gangly body pulling her across the floor, Kate has an empty space on her dance card and follows a group of guests to the dining room. On the tables, place cards identify the dishes, obviously inspired by French cuisine: *Quenelles*, some kind of meatball; *Matelot*, a strange-looking fish she can't identify; and *Croquettes*, chicken or maybe some creature from the sea mixed with rice. She starts by placing *Hâtelet*, skewered vegetables, on her plate.

"You must try the Jerusalem artichoke hearts."

He is here, after all. Standing right next to her, wearing

his smart blue uniform and a wide-open smile. The plate in her hand trembles. She places it on the table.

"On your recommendation, perhaps I shall." Those pale green eyes could easily cast a spell over her.

"Here, allow me." He scoops a few pieces from a bowl onto her plate and adds a few to his own. "The planks on Wharf Street have finally been repaired."

"Yes, I walk down that street often."

"I was so very glad to have been able to help you navigate around the hazardous debris."

"You did no such thing. I was very capable on my own." Wishing her words did not come out like daggers, she looks up at his light-hearted smile and feels foolish.

He holds his chest in a playful dramatic way. "Rebuffing my chivalry. How am I ever to recover?"

A fellow officer taps on his arm and gestures for him to join a group sitting at a table.

"May I?" He points to her dance card hanging from the ribbon around her wrist. She hands it to him.

"Miss Katherine Harding." He reads her name written on the first page. "Well, Miss Harding, it appears that I am very late in the game. Only one dance has not been reserved this entire evening. The five-step waltz." He pulls a pencil out of his jacket pocket, writes his name, and hands it back to her. "Until then." His piercing look excites her, and he leaves her to join his comrades. The table of men look over at Kate and elbow him teasingly.

She looks where he wrote his name. *Lieutenant Hugh Ashton.* Even his name is perfect. He's not a Percival or Archibald or Cornelius—all names she despises but isn't sure why.

After she finishes eating, she makes her way back to the ballroom. Mama strides up to her with serious intent.

"Where have you been? Mr. O'Brien has been looking everywhere for you."

"Am I not allowed to eat?"

"Haven't you been paying attention to your dance card? He's written himself in for the galop."

Mr. O'Brien approaches with his hand outstretched. "There she is. Quickly, Katherine, the orchestra is waiting."

Kate takes his hand and he leads her to the dance floor. Light and lively music plays and the dance begins. Mr. O'Brien is a talented dancer, which makes up for her lack of experience. Fanny galops with Philip and Emily with Henry. Papa dances with Mrs. Pemberton and Mama with Mr. Finlayson. Rebecca Thompson smiles brightly, as a smitten

Mr. Connelly twirls her around. Kate wonders if that is why Rebecca was sent to Victoria from America. To be married off to a wealthy banker. There are better odds for making a good match here, with so many gold-rich men and so few women.

When the dance is over, she checks her card. The five-step waltz is next. She looks around but doesn't see Lieutenant Ashton.

"Miss Katherine Harding," Hugh whispers behind her, his lips almost touching her ear. The tingling down her neck feels like thousands of delightful tiny pinpricks. She turns around and he offers her his arm.

As they waltz, he pulls her closer. Are they too close? She looks around but doesn't see any offended looks. He is a more tentative and less assured dancer than Mr. O'Brien, but she would far rather be in his arms than anyone else's.

His gaze doesn't leave her face.

"You are staring at me, Mr. Ashton."

"Your eyes. I have never seen such a color before. Like a periwinkle flower."

Kate looks down. She wills her cheeks from blushing, but to no avail. No man has paid this kind of attention to her. Except, of course, Mr. O'Brien.

"You are definitely one of the most beautiful women at this ball."

*One* of the most beautiful? Who else does he find attractive? Has Rebecca Thompson caught his eye? Of course she has, with her golden locks, shapely figure, and heart-warming smile.

"Beauty isn't everything, Mr. Ashton."

He chuckles. "I would expect such a response from you."

"And what would make you say that?" Again, her words tumble out her mouth, sharp as blades. "You don't even know me." She breathes deeply—must learn to control herself.

"You remind me of my sister, Julia. She fancies herself a bluestocking—very independent, intellectual, and opinionated."

"Are women not to have an intellect or opinions?" Mr. Ashton's shine is beginning to tarnish.

"Please do not misunderstand me, Miss Harding. I believe most definitely that women have a right to pursue intellectual endeavors and express their opinions. I'm just afraid society may not yet be ready to accept this."

"You are quite right on that point." His shine has been restored—in fact, it's even brighter. Perhaps he is a man who might understand her ambitions, her longings. The very depth of her soul. As they continue circling around the dance floor, it's her turn to stare. He's tall, but her hand doesn't have to reach too far to rest on his shoulder, and his physique is trim but not wiry like Philip. His eyes are perfectly symmetrical on his clean-shaven face, but his nose sits slightly to one side. She has an overwhelming urge to run her fingers through his brown wavy hair and plant a kiss on his full lips. Her first kiss.

The dance is over far too soon. With her arm in his, Hugh leads her off the dance floor.

"Thank you for the pleasure of this dance," he says. When he kisses her hand, a warm fire sizzles its way up her arm and across her chest. He looks at her with those mesmerizing eyes. "Until we meet again."

"I will look forward to it, Mr. Ashton." She watches him walk to the other side of the room to join the group of blue uniforms.

The orchestra stops and Mr. O'Brien stands in the middle of the empty dance floor.

"I would like to thank everyone for coming this evening, and I do hope a good time was had by all." Everyone claps. "It was my pleasure to host such a fine-looking group of fellow Victorians. Speaking of which ..." O'Brien looks around for Kate and, when he spots her, he holds out his hand to her.

"Katherine, would you do me the honor, as it is the last dance of the evening? A waltz, of course," he says with a wheezy chuckle.

Everyone in the entire ballroom turns to face her, including Hugh. She's mortified O'Brien has singled her out in this manner, and in front of the entire society of Victoria. She scans the expectant faces but remains frozen in place. Mama's heels click across the floor. She grips Kate's arm strongly and nudges her toward the center of the room. Kate slowly makes her way toward O'Brien. When she finally takes O'Brien's hand, the orchestra starts up, but it's only the two of them on the floor. He spins her round and round. With her eyes closed she imagines it is Hugh's hand firmly around her waist, holding her hand and guiding her confidently across the floor. After several turns around the floor, she opens her eyes. The dance floor is now full, with very few people sitting out. She skims the crowd of dancers to locate Hugh.

He is waltzing with the beautiful Rebecca.

Housemaids scurry around to deliver coats as the guests leave the ball. O'Brien says goodbye to Kate and her parents at the door.

"Thank you again, Eamonn," Papa says. "It was a delightful evening."

"My pleasure, I assure you," O'Brien says. "Before you leave, a Christmas gift for you, Katherine." He hands her a box covered in shiny silver Christmas wrap. She's at least thankful it's larger than a ring box.

"What a thoughtful thing to do, Mr. O'Brien," Mama says. "Isn't that right, Katherine?"

She hesitantly accepts it. "Yes. Thoughtful."

"Please, open it now," O'Brien says. "I want to see the look on your face."

With guests saying their goodnights around her, she unwraps the present. Inside is an emerald necklace with matching earrings. Kate is sure this extravagance is supposed to somehow guarantee the engagement. She wishes she could refuse the gift. The indifferent look on her face is not what O'Brien had hoped for.

Mama's face, however, glows as if a bolt of lightning had hit her. "Those gems are stunning,"

"Thank you," Kate says, and quickly walks down the steps to the waiting carriage.

# Chapter 8

"What did I tell you both?" Mama thrashes the soup and slams the lid on the pot as she lectures Kate and Mrs. Fleming. "That the Indian girl would leave us as fast as she arrived. That's what."

"Mama, it's only been one day. Perhaps Lucy is ill." An empty canoe floating in the harbor jumps into Kate's mind, but she chases it out.

"And another thing I predicted? That James would be broken-hearted. He won't eat or go to school." The way Mama wipes her hands on her apron, you'd think she was trying to pull off her fingers.

"I'm sure there's a logical explanation, Louisa. Katherine and will I go to the reserve right now to solve this mystery." Mrs. Fleming sounds contrite, but she has no reason to be. Although her cooking could use some improvement, Lucy has been a good housemaid for the family.

"The only mystery is why I agreed to hire that girl in the first place," Mama says.

Cupboard doors slam behind them, as Kate and Mrs. Fleming make their way down the hall to the front door.

The sky is overcast but the breeze is warm for an early January day, as they stroll toward the water's edge near Laurel Point. There is much traffic in the harbor. Steamboats and ships vie for space with Indian canoes, filled with goods and passengers heading for the Songish village or the wharf.

"Natives live a seasonal life," Mrs. Fleming says. "Sometimes they leave domestic service for a short while to hunt, fish, or harvest plants, such as camas. Other times they leave altogether without notice. There is no keeping them. They are like wild birds."

Although Kate has begged Papa to take her with him to the Songish Village, when he's been asked there to attend to a patient, he's told her it was no place for a young girl, but he has not told her why. She hears the drumming and chanting from across the water, and sees the sky lit up with open fires, especially when many other Indian nations join together for the potlatch—which in Chinook jargon means "to give away." But the village is still a mystery.

One ship enters the harbor while another leaves. Without the sails up, Kate can't tell if either one is the HMS *Forward*. Having not laid eyes on Hugh since O'Brien's ball over a month ago, she hopes he's on the ship with its bow pointing toward Victoria.

A Songish man is waiting on the point to paddle them across. Unlike Old Pierre, his hair is cropped short, and he wears wool trousers and a matching jacket. Mrs. Fleming greets him. She appears to be quite fluent in the Lekwammen language. But for all Kate knows, they could be speaking Chinook jargon.

"Katherine, this is Johnny."

He nods and offers Kate his dark leathery hand as she steps into the canoe. As she shifts to the front, it tips from side to side. He says something, points to the center of the dugout boat, as he sloshes through the icy water beside the canoe to guide her steps. Mrs. Fleming, who is used to riding in canoes, holds the sides as she climbs in and squats in the middle. Other than the annual May picnics boating north of the Indian village, Kate rarely gets the chance to be on the water. Both ships have now vacated the waterway, so they have a clear passage across to the reserve. The canoe scrapes on the small rocks as Johnny pushes off, hops in the back, and begins paddling. The gentle rocking and swaying and the sounds of waves lapping soothe her. But the thought of paddling alone in icy winter storms, or in the dead of night like Lucy does almost every day, is beyond her comprehension.

As they get closer to the village, a head pops up out of the water. When the bird fully surfaces, Kate recognizes the loon's black and white checker back. Her disturbing dream comes to mind when the bird cocks its head and observes her closely with its red eyes. It calls out a haunting hooting sound followed by a high-pitched yodel, like a scream. Johnny says something to Mrs. Fleming. Kate looks over her shoulder to see a grin on his face.

"He says you must listen to the loon. It's trying to tell you something." The man nods and chuckles softly to himself as he dips the paddle into the water.

The bird continues to swim right beside Kate at the front of the canoe, its beady eye still fixed on her. *What is it you need to tell me?* It dives back under the water, leaving Kate unsettled.

Several other dugout canoes line the shore of the small inlet. As they approach the beach, Johnny steps out into the water and guides the canoe to dry land. He offers his hand to

Kate; her boots make a crunching sound when she steps onto the stony beach. She's shocked to see three naked men by the water, scrubbing themselves with cedar boughs—and right in front of women and children. She has caught glimpses of miners outside their tents with their shirts off, but never before has she seen a man completely unclothed. Only in the illustrations in Mr. Gray's anatomy book. This must be the reason why Papa hasn't wanted her to accompany him on his rounds here. And if Mama were not so desperate for a housemaid, she would not have allowed her to come, either.

"Eyes ahead, Katherine," Mrs. Fleming says.

She must have been staring.

Just ahead, two women in skirts and blouses carry baskets on their backs. A thin strap around their foreheads bears the weight of the load. Kate has seen Indian women in town, carrying baskets of fish, shellfish, and potatoes. She can't imagine the stress on those women's bodies, walking through the streets of Victoria with such heavy cargo.

"They have fresh clams for sale," Mrs. Fleming says. "Shall we buy some later for you to take home? They're delicious steamed in vegetable broth."

Mama has never had clams on her dinner menu, even though they are easy to purchase from the Indians.

Several rectangular buildings made of cedar planks line the shore and bluffs, and the air smells of the smoke that rises from holes in the roof. Some are small shacks, whose wooden boards look haphazardly nailed together. Others are larger structures—bigger and taller than her home—supported with large wooden posts. Outside of these buildings, long strips of fish hang to dry.

As Kate follows Mrs. Fleming to the center of the village, a barking white dog running toward them startles her.

"Did you know the Songish women breed these dogs?"

"I know very little about the Songish people, I'm afraid." Other than what she reads in *The British Colonist* or overhears from adult conversations during social gatherings. And it is usually a negative perspective.

"The women shear the dogs and spin their wool. The more dogs a woman owns, the wealthier she appears. Look in this house."

Inside, a woman draped in a blanket weaves at a loom. The large mat on which she sits must have been woven out of cedar, as the scent in the room indicates. Beside her, a baby is swaddled and strapped into a wooden frame, while a small naked boy plays with a fluffy white puppy. Blankets are stacked in one corner.

"With all those blankets, I'm curious if they are preparing for another potlatch," Mrs. Fleming says. "Much more is given away at potlatches besides the blankets—canoes, slaves, woodcarvings ... They are a very generous people."

"Papa was given one of the Songish blankets for seeing a patient on the reserve. It's draped over a chair in his surgery." One of the reasons their family is in such financial difficulties. Papa waives his fees if people cannot pay. He once brought home sacks of turnips and apples after visiting a farmer. Most likely the only payment he accepted.

"The warp is made out of thin strips of cedar bark, and the weft is woven mainly from the dog's fur, but also partly from mountain-goat wool, traded from the Squamish and Nooksack," Mrs. Fleming says. "Woven with such great care. I fail to understand why Indians are so enamored with Hudson's Bay blankets, when what they create is so much lovelier."

On a path between buildings, women weave baskets out of long, thin cedar strips. Another large lodge is divided into several compartments, with what looks like platforms on which to sleep. Sitting on the ground, men play some kind of game, shuffling circular wooden pieces.

"*Lehallum*, a gambling game," Mrs. Fleming says. "There

is no doubt they are passionate about their gambling. Sometimes they pass two or three consecutive days and nights without ceasing. I once heard of a man who wagered and lost his canoe, worth one hundred dollars."

Gambling. One more reason Mama believes the Indian life is riddled with iniquity. It is only a game. Other than risking losing personal possessions, is anyone harmed? Perhaps they are.

Further down, a man carves animal shapes out of a small log. Cheealthluc, the Songish chief, who is also known as King Freezy, strides toward them with a big smile. His head of hair and beard are bushy. As usual, he wears an old navy uniform. Kate often sees him around town with his queen and entourage. He and Mrs. Fleming share words.

"I know your father," he says to Kate.

"Yes, Papa has visited your village." As a last resort, Cheealthluc occasionally calls on Papa for medical assistance.

"Good man," Cheealthluc says.

"Indeed, he is," Kate says.

"Good day to you, Cheealthluc," Mrs. Fleming says, as they continue to walk through the village to a smaller plank home. "This is where Lucy's family lives." At the door, an elderly stout woman with bare legs and only a blanket to cover her shoulders, talks with Mrs. Fleming. Only dirt covers the floors. Woven fabric hangings divide the large open area into rooms. One of the curtains pulls away and Lucy, with her hair plaited in several braids close to her scalp, smiles shyly at Kate. And like the older woman, only a blanket covers her. Kate waves at Lucy, so relieved to see her. Lucy waves back.

"Is Lucy unwell?" Kate asks.

"No, her great-aunty tells me it's her first menses. She must work here in the mornings and rest in the afternoons until it has ceased."

"Does this mean she will be absent for service every month?"

"No, just the first time."

Kate is thankful for that, since it would infuriate Mama if this were to be a monthly occurrence. Kate remembers being terrified of imminent death when she first saw blood trickle from between her legs. It was Papa who explained to her that menses is a natural womanly function. Maybe Lucy would want to talk to her to ease any fears she may have.

Other than work and rest, Kate wonders what else the Indians do to mark this passage of life?

Lucy comes out from behind the curtain and hands Kate

a small doll, woven with thin cedar strips. "For James."

"Thank you, Lucy. He misses you very much. We all do."

Lucy nods and goes back behind her curtain.

Back at the beach, Kate and Mrs. Fleming buy bags of clams before they board the canoe. Johnny pushes them off and starts paddling. On the ride back, Kate searches for the loon, but it doesn't appear.

When Kate arrives home, Mama is relieved that she won't have to train a new housemaid. Kate carries a tray of food upstairs to James, who is holed up in his room. She finds him curled up in his bed, covers pulled under his chin and big eyes wide open.

"I brought your favorite—a slice of ham and cheese with peasant bread from the bakery."

"I am not hungry."

She places the tray on the dresser, and then pulls the cedar doll out of her pocket and shows it to James.

James shoots up to sitting. "What is that?"

"A present from Lucy."

James grabs it. "You saw her? Where is she? Is she ever coming back to our house?"

"Lucy is at her home. She needs to stay with her family

for a few days, but she'll be back with us soon."

A smile crosses James's face as he carefully inspects the doll. "Lucy must teach me how to make one just like this."

"Hungry now?"

She puts the tray on his bed, watches him bite into the thick crust of bread, as he happily plays with the doll.

She goes to her room, sees an envelope on her desk. She rips open the letter from Arthur.

*London*
*30th Sept '61*

*Dearest Kate,*

*My life has not improved since I last wrote to you. In fact, it has gotten much worse in many ways. I am failing my medical studies horribly. Has the letter from St. George's arrived for Papa, telling him that I'm on academic probation? If my marks don't improve drastically by the end of the term, which is very soon, I will be asked to leave the university and give up my seat to a more worthy candidate. Papa will lose the cost of tuition for the entire year, which pains me a great deal.*

*I am the author of my own demise, as they say. Rather than attending classes, I have been spending my days sketching artifacts at museums or any human form in front of me, or studying painting techniques at galleries. I am a lost soul, Kate, living out my lie wandering the streets of London. And I do not know where to turn. I did hear of an artist colony in Paris to which I might escape. With the city's many art schools and exhibition places, painters and sculptors from all over the world are flocking there. How could I afford to live such a life in Paris? I do not know. But how can I afford not to follow my heart that is pulling me there?*

*I think of you often, my dear Kate.*

*Your loving brother,*

*Arthur*

Out her bedroom window, an ugly storm cloud, the color of a bruise, hangs in the sky. Although Kate feels badly and, yes, disappointed in her brother, she wishes with every cell in her body that she could be the worthy candidate to take his place for medical studies. But how could she replace him? Would St. George's ever accept a female student? The tuition would already be paid. She could dress as a man. Like Hannah Snell, the Englishwoman who, in 1748, assumed the identity of her brother-in-law and served in the Royal Marines for four years before her gender was discovered.

As Mama puts James to bed, Kate finishes drying the last dish after a steamed clam dinner. She was surprised how much Mama embraced the shellfish bought from the reserve. The thought of soon having Lucy back had lifted Mama's spirits. Out the window, Kate sees a dim light in Papa's surgery. She hangs up her apron, and carries a lit candle down the narrow hallway to the back of the house.

She finds Papa, as usual, puffing on his pipe, while writing his patient notes.

"Kitty, my dear. I saw that you finally returned my medical notes. I wondered if I would see my booklet ever again." He taps out the spent ashes from his pipe and fills it with fresh tobacco.

"Papa, ask me questions."

"Questions? What about?"

"About the medicines."

"Kitty ..." He lights his pipe with the long tapered candle on his desk.

"Please, Papa."

He takes a few puffs. The sweet-smelling smoke curls and dances in the air.

"Myrrh," he finally says.

"It is used in diseases characterized by feebleness of the muscular fiber and vascular action," she says.

"Belladonna."

"It allays pain and irritation and ..." she searches her memory, "rubbed on the skin is its most valuable application."

Papa nods, sucks in the smoke and blows it out. "Camphor."

"It relieves nervous and hysterical depression. It can also be used for pain and restlessness of the nervous system."

"Well done, Kitty."

"I'm not finished. Camphor is also of good service in low fevers and spasmodic diseases."

With a big smile, Papa sticks his pipe in his teeth and claps his hands. This may be the only recognition she will receive for her passion and hard work, but she will take it.

In her bedroom, Kate brushes out her long black hair, taming the curls as best she can with a sprinkle of water from a glass. She looks at herself closely in the mirror—the dark night to Rebecca Thompson's sunny day. She wonders which Lieutenant Hugh Ashton would prefer. If it were up to her, she would take bright sun over gloomy darkness any day. The box with O'Brien's emeralds sits on the dresser. She puts down her brush and opens it. She can't deny the jewelry is exquisite. She imagines herself as O'Brien's wife, with a jewelry cabinet full of sparkling gems. She quickly closes the box and stuffs it in a bottom drawer behind her stockings.

She snuffs out the candle and buries herself under the heavy cover on her bed, as the last of the logs in the fireplace crackles. She considers where Hugh is at this very moment. Sailing the Pacific Ocean, heading to South America. Or Polynesia. Maybe on the ship anchored in Victoria's harbor. Or out at a saloon in town with his comrades. She wills him to be in Victoria, close by, and soon falls asleep.

*She walks through a forest carpeted with moss and ferns. Hears the eerie screech of the loon echoing through the ancient trees. Reaches the shoreline where the loon is bobbing in the waves. The loon wants her to follow. She doesn't feel the water's icy chill, as the loon leads her deeper and deeper, her dress floating up around her. The water is over her head, her body submerged. The loon dives down and circles her. Circles again and again. She can't hold her breath any longer. Frantically she flails her arms, kicks her legs, but she can't reach the surface. Sinks deeper. The loon swims closer. She feels a sharp sting from its piercing red eye pinch her heart.*

Kate's eyes shoot open. It's the black of night.

# Chapter 9

Kate, still reeling from her dream from the night before, lifts her skirt as her rubber boots slosh and suck down into the wet pebbly beach near Ogden Point. The sound of horns from ships, hidden behind the dense fog blanketing the Strait of Juan de Fuca, reverberates across the water. The air is pungent with salt and seaweed on the low tide beach. James and Lucy, both carrying buckets, happily splash through the water that is still receding.

"Lucy, is there a Songish story of the loon?" Kate asks.

Lucy looks at her questioningly.

"I have had two dreams now about a loon. Disturbing dreams. As if the loon were stalking me in my sleep like a wild animal."

Lucy walks in silence. James runs ahead, splashing and swinging his bucket.

"What do you make of these dreams?" Kate asks.

Lucy gathers her thoughts. Seems reluctant to speak, as if she might be telling a secret. "*Skwinonet*."

"What does that mean?"

"The loon may be your *skwinonet*—spirit helper. They come in dreams."

"But what is this spirit helper trying to tell me?"

"To pay heed."

"Pay heed to what?"

"To what you most wish for." Lucy gives her a grave look. "If you don't, you will be ... haunted."

Kate is taken aback. "Haunted?"

Lucy nods. Hearing this story unsettles Kate. What she most wishes for, becoming a doctor, may never come to pass. Is her fate to be haunted the rest of her life?

A wailing sea gull flies overhead, drops a clam from its beak. It smashes on the beach along with a pile of broken shells.

"James, here," Lucy says, dropping to her knees. He comes running back, as she scrapes the top of the pebbly muck with a long flat oyster shell.

"I see one." James excitedly sinks his hands into the mud and pulls out a clam.

"Look." Lucy points to a tiny hole in the sand where water squirts out.

James digs around further, picks up a few more clams, and plops them into his bucket. "Mama will be so proud that we are bringing dinner home." He looks up at Kate with big eyes. "Won't she, Kate?"

"Of course she will." But Kate isn't so sure. James is already soaking wet and covered in mud, which she knows Mama will disapprove of.

"Near reserve is better." Lucy pushes aside the sand with the shell.

"Then why can we not dig for clams there?" James asks.

"My family don't own it."

"Own what, Lucy?" Kate asks.

"Land for clams is passed down from ancestors."

"What does your family own?" James asks.

"Camas fields."

"Are you rich, Lucy?" James asks.

"No, *stesem*. Not rich, not slave."

Kate has heard about the Songish class system. They are called barbaric for exploiting slaves won in battles with other tribes. But what about so-called civilized societies? England, Spain, and Portugal have a long history of buying, selling, and working slaves. And, according to what she has read in *The British Colonist*, slavery is one of the main causes of the civil war in the United States, that began almost a year ago and still rages on. Indentured servants have been sent to work land on Vancouver Island for gentlemen landowners, which in Kate's mind is slavery.

"You try it, Kate," James says. Lucy hands her the oyster shell.

Kate rolls up her coat sleeves, squats down, and digs with the shell. She uncovers several more clams, picks them up, and brushes them off. The cold, gritty sand feels soothing. She kneels down, buries both hands into the ground, feels around for more clams. She shuts her eyes, lets the cool breeze caress her face.

When the buckets are almost filled, Kate stands and brushes the beach off her skirt, which is not only dirty, but also sopping wet where she knelt. Down the way, phantom shapes move toward them through the fog. Male voices echo off the bluffs. Soon a group of men appears out of the mist. A few stop to skip rocks in the water. As they get closer, Kate sees Hugh. Her whole body vibrates. A strand of hair refuses to be pinned back. She quickly pinches her cheeks to pink up her pale complexion.

"He is pretty," Lucy says quietly to Kate.

"Miss Harding. What a surprise," Hugh says, walking

toward her, wearing a smart brown day suit. His chums, also in civilian clothing, tip their hats to her and continue down the beach.

Kate is suddenly mortified. What a state she must look with her wild hair and soiled skirt.

She curtseys. "Good day, Mr. Ashton. Or should I call you Lieutenant Ashton?"

"Please, just call me Hugh. And may I call you Katherine?"

"If you like. Most people call me Kate, except my mama who calls me Katherine, but my papa has called me Kitty ever since I remember." Her tongue is keeping time to her beating heart. *Stop it.*

Hugh reaches out and gently brushes her cheek with his thumb. "Well, Kate, it appears you are wearing half the beach on your face."

Of course, when she pinched her cheeks. What a fool she is.

"Are you really a Lieutenant?" James asks, covered in sand and looking like a ragamuffin.

"Yes, I am. Lieutenant Hugh Ashton, at your service," he says, first saluting then holding out his hand for James to shake. "And you are?"

"James Sebastian William Harding," he says, shaking hands. "I'm Kate's brother." When Hugh runs his hand down the side of his trousers, Kate is sure he's wiping off the grit from James's hand. "Are you an army Lieutenant or a navy Lieutenant? And why are you not in uniform?"

"Navy. The HMS *Forward*. And the Captain sometimes allows the officers leave."

"Will you take me aboard your ship someday? I would ever so like to see inside," James says.

"James, don't be so forward." Kate turns to Hugh. "I apologize for my brother."

"No apology necessary." To James. "If there is ever a possibility, I would be delighted to take you on a tour of the ship." His green eyes turn to Kate. "Perhaps your sister could come along, too." At that moment, she would follow that handsome face anywhere, even to the ends of the Earth.

"Come," Lucy says to James, picking up the buckets and starting down the beach. She turns and smiles at Kate.

While the other men continue down the beach, Hugh gestures to a log for them to sit.

"Will your ship be stationed in Esquimalt for long?" Kate has heard of young women falling in love with officers, only to have them sail off for Asia, Africa, or China and never return. Not that she plans on falling in love, of course.

"One never knows when the order will come to leave on

another mission. We are stationed here for now, but at sea most of the time."

"Defending English interests, I presume?"

"As you must know, there have been tensions with the United States since the Oregon Treaty was signed. With the coal and gold discovered in the colony, there's much to protect. And, of course, there are always problems to resolve with hostile natives."

Kate has heard about the Kwakiutl, Nootka, and Tlingit villages, destroyed by naval bombardment or burned to the ground, in response to ships being attacked or the killing of settlers. Although she feels the naval retaliation was overly harsh, she doesn't want to say anything and risk losing his favor. Kate often watches Indian canoes navigate their way to and from the village around boats and ships at the mouth of the harbor. Will the navy have to subdue the Songish in the same way at some point? The thought makes Kate shudder inside.

"How long have you been at sea?" Kate asks.

"The ship sailed from Liverpool four years ago, after I completed my naval training."

"Where is your family from?"

"Cambridge, but my three brothers and I went to boarding school in Berkshire."

He is obviously from a fairly wealthy family that could afford to send four boys away to school. If this acquaintance ever came to anything, this would definitely please Mama.

"And I know you are from London," he says.

"Did my accent give me away?"

"No, I have spies in town." Hugh smiles, raises his eyebrows up and down playfully.

"Is that so? What else did your spies tell you about my family?"

"That if I break a bone or fall ill with any disease, your father is one of the preferred doctors in Victoria. Also, you have an older brother at university in London."

"Not much more to tell, I'm afraid. My world is very small and tedious."

"And I also heard ... that a marriage proposal from Mr. O'Brien is imminent."

"No such proposal has been offered or accepted," Kate says emphatically, hoping she is making it clear to Hugh she is not taken. At least, not yet.

"I am only conveying what is rumored around the town."

"What other stories have your spies told you about me?"

Hugh's handsome smile disarms her. "Despite handing over large sums of money, that's all I could glean."

A fellow officer whistles and gestures for Hugh to join them.

"But it appears I will have to wait to continue this conversation. Do you need me to escort you home?"

"No, but I thank you for your kindness."

Hugh offers Kate his hand and helps her to standing. Instead of letting go, he pulls her close. He smells sweet, like vanilla. When he kisses her hand, the warmth of his lips radiates up her arm. He stares right into her eyes for a long moment. "Until we meet again."

He jogs down the beach to join his friends. It must have appeared at the Christmas ball that Kate's fate was sealed in marriage to Mr. O'Brien. Does she really not have a say in her own future? She laments at the thought of the HMS *Forward* sailing away on another mission, far away from Vancouver Island.

She opens the front door to hear her parents' voices in the sitting room. Mama sounds upset. Kate hangs up her coat, brushes off the remaining sand from her skirt, and makes her way down the hall.

Mama is crying, wiping tears with her hankie. Papa is pacing, with a severe look on his face.

"Has something happened?" Kate asks.

"It is Arthur," Mama says, sniffling and wiping her nose. "He has failed his studies and is now being asked to leave St. George's. A disgrace to our family's name. What will we tell people?"

"He has been writing to only you, Kitty," Papa says. "Has he mentioned anything about this?"

"He ... he wrote to me he hasn't been happy lately. With his studies, that is."

"Whatever do you mean?" Mama says.

She doesn't know how much to reveal. It is up to Arthur to explain himself. But she can't go back now.

"He is most sure that medicine is not his professional calling."

"His calling is to follow his papa into a respectable profession, and that is that," Mama says.

"Now, Louisa. That isn't helping the matter." Papa turns to Kate. "Please tell us what you know."

"It's not my story to tell, Papa. You will hear from Arthur soon enough, I assure you." Papa continues pacing, rubbing his temples.

"You tell us everything, Katherine," Mama says.

"I have told you as much as I know. I am sure he will write to you."

"All that money for his tuition will never be recovered. Never," Mama says, blowing her nose. "What are we to do now?"

Kate doesn't want to think about the enormous financial cost to her family. Nor does she want to ruminate about how, in a different world, she could have been the beneficiary of that university education, and would not have squandered even one farthing. She leaves, goes up the stairs to her room.

Sitting at her desk, she dips her pen in the inkwell.

*Katherine Harding*
*2 Kingston Street*
*Victoria, Colony of Vancouver Island*

*15th January 1862*

*Miss Elizabeth Blackwell*
*New York Infirmary for Poor Women and Children*
*New York City, New York*
*United States of America*

*Dear Miss Blackwell,*

*I hope with all of my heart that this letter*

*finds you. I know only the name of your infirmary in New York City, and that is all.*

*My thoughts have been swirling like a tidal pool since I heard of your existence. My friend, Sister Mary Providence, told me of your brave pioneering spirit in the field of medicine. Your challenging of such a formidable male domain—the medical faculty at a New York university—has been an enormous inspiration to me. And to hear you graduated top of your class gives me great satisfaction, indeed. The only woman in the United States, and possibly the entire world for all I know, to receive a medical degree.*

*I am the daughter of a physician and have been fascinated with the medical profession since I was a young child, first growing up in London and now on the Colony of Vancouver Island. I, too, have a sharp intellect and graduated top of my class at St. Ann's School here in Victoria. However, I have been brought up to believe that the narrow domestic sphere is the only path to which a woman can ever aspire. I must tell you, Miss Blackwell, the thought of living such a constricted life has led me down a dark abyss of despair. My mind is excruciatingly curious and, like you, my heart is pulling me to the medical profession. But, alas, so much of life conspires against my desire to follow your lead.*

*Surely you must have had similar longings and impossible challenges. If you have any advice for a desperate young woman, I would be most grateful to receive a letter back from you.*

*Yours with the deepest respect,*

*Katherine Harding*

# Chapter 10

Kate assists Mama as she steps up into the carriage. Papa is seeing patients in the surgery today, so the horse and carriage are available. Kate climbs into the box seat beside her mama and picks up the reins. "Walk on, Nora." Kate eases the reins.

The carriage lurches forward down the muddy road. Mama's black mourning dress looks tired and worn. Since receiving the news from St. George's about Arthur's academic catastrophe almost a week ago, Mama has barely said a word to anyone. She hasn't received any guests and has spent most days in her room, only coming out for meals. Another bout of grieving that has been inflicted on the family. The house has been as quiet as a graveyard.

"It's a lovely day, is it not, Mama?" Although the clouds are trimmed with charcoal gray, the salty ocean breeze feels almost warm for a January day.

"I suppose it is." Mama doesn't sound so sure.

It took much convincing from Kate for Mama to finally accept the invitation to Mrs. Bennet's tea party, to present her niece Rebecca to Victoria society ladies. Although Kate is sure Emily and Fanny will be there, and she will have to endure an afternoon of mindless conversation, she is intrigued to meet Rebecca. If only to find out if she might have any romantic interest in Hugh. But what does that matter, really? He's probably already back on his ship, out to sea, far away from the both of them.

"I trust you will not say one word to anyone about Arthur," Mama says.

"You know I would not, Mama." But it's only a matter of time before all Harding acquaintances, here and abroad, will know the story in exaggerated detail.

They bypass the bridge into town and, instead, Nora sloshes through the mud on the rugged trail on the edge of James Bay, toward McClure Street. They meander through the streets, the roads lined with empty lots, farming plots, and a few houses with barren winter gardens. Two-wheeled carts carrying large barrels pass by them, hauling water from Spring Ridge into town. They turn down the public road toward Oak Bay, where the Bennets live on a grand estate outside of town. In the distance, Mount Baker's snowy winter peak shoots up through the clouds, across the strait in the Washington Territory.

They finally arrive at the Bennets' stately home, surrounded by tall pine and birch trees stripped of their leaves. Han, the Chinese houseboy, greets them at the door and shows them in. Unlike many Chinamen in town, who wear traditional garb, Han's hair is cut short, and he wears a smart black day suit with a crisp white shirt, buttoned to the top.

"Mrs. Harding, so nice of you to come," Mrs. Bennet says. "And Katherine, what a pleasure." Han begins to pour tea and hands cups to Mrs. Fleming, Mrs. Pemberton, and Mrs. Finlayson, seated by the fireplace, already in conversation. Fanny and Emily sit in a circle of chairs, looking in awe as Rebecca, wearing a royal blue dress with white polka dots, animatedly entertains them with a story. Golden curls spill down her back. Kate looks at her own gray dress and thinks it awfully drab, despite the delicate white lace collar.

"Rebecca, dear," Mrs. Bennet calls her niece over. "I'd like to introduce you to Mrs. Harding and her daughter, Katherine."

The three women curtsey and say their "How do you do's."

"Are you related to Dr. Harding?" Rebecca asks.

"Why, yes, he is my husband. I hope you have not been in need of his medical attention since you arrived in Victoria."

"No, but I did have an engaging conversation with him at Mr. O'Brien's ball, about the history of Fort Victoria and the Hudson's Bay Company. A charming man."

"Indeed." Mama looks surprised that this bold young woman considers her husband charming.

Rebecca loops her arm around Kate's. "Come, Katherine, let's get acquainted." Kate notices that Emily and Fanny look hurt when Rebecca guides her to the window seat at the opposite end of the room.

"I don't know whether or not you are dear friends of Fanny and Emily, but neither have read Voltaire. Please tell me you have read *Candide*."

"Indeed, I have."

"Oh, thank heaven." Rebecca lets out an enormous sigh. "If I have to hear one more intricate detail of a doily or silver tea service, or petit-point tapestry tablecloth that has been added to their trousseau chests, I would surely put heavy rocks in my pockets and walk out into the ocean."

Kate is both intrigued by Rebecca and taken aback by her haughty tone. "They are my friends, although not close. They mean well, even if their horizons tend to be fairly narrow." Kate is surprised at how strongly she feels she must defend Fanny and Emily to Rebecca.

"I'm so sorry if I offended you or them. My Manhattan snobbery comes all too naturally, I'm afraid. But I do long for stimulating discourse."

So does Kate. Desperately. They glance over at Emily and Fanny, who are now helping themselves to the tray of pastries.

"When I first saw you at the ball," Rebecca continues, "I knew you would be someone I could truly relate to in this tiny speck of a town. You have a stoic, refined air about you, which immediately intrigued me." Rebecca's round brown eyes look deeply into hers. "Like you have some dark secrets of the soul."

Kate is both shocked and refreshed by Rebecca's direct manner.

"First of all, please call me Kate."

"Kate. What a terribly romantic name. Sorry if I come across too fiercely—I've been told I'm as subtle as a typhoon. But don't you feel that there is never a moment of time to waste? This stream of life we are floating down is so ephemeral, don't you think? The past is already a ghost, the present far too short, and the future never arrives." Her brow folds into a serious furrow and her eyes are intense and pleading.

"Yes, I do feel that way. Quite often, actually."

Rebecca takes her hands. "I just knew we would be kindred spirits."

Kate feels excitedly unsteady—she has never met anyone quite like Rebecca.

"Tell me one thing I simply *must* know about you," Rebecca says.

The warmth of Rebecca's hands feels soothing. What Kate wants to say is that she feels desperately alone in this tiny speck of a town, as Rebecca calls it. But instead she says, "There is truly not much to tell."

"I highly doubt that, Miss Katherine Harding." When Rebecca smiles, it's like a bright sun opening up Kate's gloomy skies.

"Tell me about you?" Kate asks.

"The one thing you must know is I was sent away from New York City to live with my aunt ..." Rebecca looks around and lowers her voice, "to escape a scandal."

"A scandal you were involved in?"

Rebecca nods. Kate is now even more intrigued with this new friend.

"Rebecca, my dear," Mrs. Bennet says, "Mrs. Finlayson would like to chat with you before she has to take her leave."

"Of course, Aunt Clara." Mrs. Bennet gives Rebecca an admonishing gaze, turns to join the others. Rebecca whispers to Kate. "She will not abide my sordid story being told. May we continue this conversation in private, at a later date?"

"Most definitely."

Rebecca gently squeezes her hands, stands, and goes to where the group of women, including Mama, are sitting.

Fanny and Emily sit on either side of Kate on the window seat.

"What do you think of Rebecca?" Emily says, licking the cream filling from the center of her pastry.

"She is rather peculiar, is she not?" Fanny says.

"Yes, she is," Kate says. Snobbery aside, she is Kate's kind of peculiar. She watches the ladies' rapt expressions as Rebecca charms them with a story.

Rebecca's possible romantic intentions with Hugh don't cross her mind until the carriage ride home. And even though she knows so little of Rebecca, she thinks Hugh would be a fool not to pursue a courtship with such a beautiful, vibrant, fascinating woman. But then again, whatever the scandal Rebecca finds herself in may prevent any attachments.

Kate places a bowl of soup, a slice of bread, and a cup of tea on a tray, while Lucy stacks clean dinner dishes into the cupboards.

"Is she ill?" Lucy asks.

"Mama received difficult news today from my brother in England. She is taking it very hard. And Papa is out on a call in Sooke—tonight of all nights."

Lucy opens a tin container, scoops out a piece of cake, and puts it on a plate. She places the plate on the tray.

"That is thoughtful of you, Lucy."

Mama sits by the window in her bedroom, clutching Arthur's letter.

"Mama, here is some soup for you, and Lucy made your favorite apple cake." She places the tray on the chest of drawers.

Mama looks at her blankly. "How could I eat at a time like this?"

"But, Mama, this could not have come as a surprise. You were forewarned by the letter from the university."

"To read Arthur's own words has completely and utterly broken me." She hands Kate the letter.

*London*

*5 Oct '61*

*Dear Papa and Mama,*

*It is with a dreadfully heavy heart that I write this letter to you. By now you will have received my expulsion letter from St. George's. I can only imagine the gamut of feelings you must have experienced—shock, anger, shame, sadness, disappointment. I am exceedingly sorry for putting you through such turmoil, but know that whatever you are experiencing, my anguish is infinitely greater.*

*You have always placed such great faith in me and in my academic potential. I am eternally grateful for that. I have always believed medicine is a noble calling and have been proud of Papa's career. However, even during my very first week at St. George's, I knew medicine was not my professional calling. I completed my first year, mostly out of duty to you, but knew in my heart of hearts I could not return. It was never my intention to deceive you. But it has taken until now, regrettably, after you have paid hundreds of pounds of tuition, for me to finally surrender the façade. I cannot promise that I will ever be able to pay you back all the money I owe, but know that I will do my utmost to repay whatever debt I am able.*

*You may have heard that Uncle Charles offered me a job at the London and Westminster Bank. I was forced to turn him down—I would have been trading one unfitting occupation for another. I have recently found work in a cabinetmaker's shop. I know working with my hands is not the vocation you imagined for me, but this type of work has its mental exertion as well as creative elements. The words of Francis of Assisi ring very true to me at this time.*

*He who works with his hands is a laborer.*

*He who works with his hands and his head is a craftsman.*

*He who works with his hands and his head and his heart is an artist.*

*I intend to find a vocation where I can work with my hands, head, and heart. But for now, this manual labor pays for my room and board at a lodging house where I recently moved. I will never again be in your debt; I promise you that.*

*I hope you will both find it in your hearts to forgive me, understand my impossible predicament, and support this new journey I am on, even though I have no idea where it might lead.*

*Your faithful son,*

*Arthur*

Kate sits in the chair across from Mama, places the letter on the small table between them.

"Working with his hands?" Mama shakes her head. "It is moral insanity."

"Arthur is not insane." A wave of anger and courage builds inside Kate and rises to the surface in a small explosion. "Mama, is there some way you can accept your children for who they are? Not who you think they should be?"

Mama looks surprised at Kate's assertiveness. "That is

unfair, Katherine. All I have ever wanted is what is best for my children."

"What *you* think is best. You are ruled by the fear of what others might think." Kate has never spoken so forthrightly to her mama. She feels both terrified and exhilarated. "Can you ever stop being the puppeteer controlling the strings of the marionette?"

Mama looks out the window at the black of night. Kate can tell she has struck a chord.

"I only want to dispossess you and your brothers of the notion that you have any choices in this life, because you do not, and the sooner you are aware of this the better," Mama says in a cool, even tone. "If Arthur thinks he will live well, cobbling together a meagre living working in a trade, then he is mistaken. He will live in poverty like the rest of the lower classes, struggling to feed his family."

"But it is his choice to make," Kate says.

"And for you, as a woman—barred by law and custom from entering a profession and restricted in the possession of property—marrying well is ultimately your only survival. And, yes, perhaps the survival of our family. If I am the puppeteer, I am only guiding the strings to assure a better life for you, for everyone."

"Did you ever dream of a different life? One where you were the master of your destiny?" Kate asks.

Mama is quiet for a long moment. "Before I met your papa, I wished to set up a shop importing the finest of fabrics—block printed cotton chintz from India, silks from the Orient, Brussels lace." A weak smile crosses her face. "I even found the perfect location for my shop near Haverstock Hill." She looks at Kate. "But, of course, women lack the intellect, the stamina, and competitive drive required to run a business."

"Surely you don't believe that, Mama?"

"It doesn't matter what I believe." Mama wipes away a tear.

"Would running that business not have made you the happiest of women?"

"My happiness is not important."

"But it is to me." Kate kneels at Mama's feet and takes her hands. "And it should be to you, as well."

"I will not dwell on the past, Katherine. What is done is done. I am as happy as I can ever expect to be."

The resigned look on Mama's face deeply saddens her. Kate knows from this moment forward, she will never settle in life like her mama has, even if she must face the greatest of life's challenges.

In Papa's surgery, Kate looks through the medicine chest. She picks up a bottle of Rhodium oil, shakes the mixture, and observes how the liquid settles. She refers to Papa's written text and writes the medicinal properties in her notebook. *Used to enhance energy and heightened awareness. Controls unnatural sleep disorders.* She sees Papa's patient records in a booklet on his desk. Patient records are confidential. She rests her hand on the outside of the book for a long moment. Soon, her curiosity plows over her conscience. She opens the book and begins reading the patient notes.

Heaviness and pain much diminished.

*Sleep comes more easily ... fewer sparks before the eyes. Foul taste in the mouth.*

*Bowels open freely ... pupil of right eye contracted but is obedient to light. Somewhat unresponsive to pulsing light.*

*Walks about freely with little dizziness.*

She burns down one candle and lights another, diagnosing maladies and matching them with medicines she has studied. When she hears Nora's clopping hooves pass the house, heading toward the barn, she quickly puts Papa's notes and books back exactly where she found them, closes his medicine chest, blows out the candle, and leaves the surgery.

# Chapter 11

Beams of sun pour through the stained-glass head of Jesus wearing a golden crown and a purple robe. His hand, with the nail wound of the crucifixion, is raised in blessing. Kate sits with Mama in their regular pew in the middle of the church. The wooden pew feels cold and hard under Kate. Early this morning, Papa was called out to Craigflower Farm to see to a laborer who was kicked by a horse. Kate begged to go with him, but Mama insisted she join her at church.

Sweet voices of the children's choir echo throughout the stone walls of the church.

*All things bright and beautiful,*
*All creatures great and small,*
*All things wise and wonderful*
*The Lord God made them all.*

James is supposed to be focused on Mrs. Fleming, the choir director. Instead, his eyes and attention flit around like a hummingbird. Strangely, this makes Kate's heart swell with love for her brother.

*Each little flower that opens,*
*Each little bird that sings,*
*He made their glowing colors,*
*He made their tiny wings.*

When the choir finishes their hymn, some officers from HMS *Forward* arrive late and sit in pews at the back. Kate glances over her shoulder, but her excitement turns to disappointment when she doesn't see Hugh among them. He may not belong to the Church of England. Perhaps he's Presbyterian or Lutheran. He might even be Catholic.

"I have a soul as well as a body," Reverend Fleming's sermon from his pulpit begins. "My soul must live forever in happiness or misery. It is capable of pain or pleasure inconceivably greater than my body."

Kate dwells on her own soul. Never mind the afterlife; not fulfilling her soul's destiny on Earth might cause her the greatest of pain and misery. But she's still unsure what her destiny is to be. Marry Hugh and be left running a house full of his children, while he sails the seven seas. Marry Mr. O'Brien, a man she is indifferent to, but someone who could ensure her entire family would want for nothing ever again. What about her impossible dream of becoming a doctor? Is that her true destiny?

"It is a matter of little importance whether I am in abject poverty or the greatest affluence during the few years I am to continue in the present world," the Reverend continues. "Whether I am respected or despised by my fellow mortals, whether my body is sickly or healthy, painful or at ease ..."

Kate looks near the front of the church where Rebecca sits with Mr. and Mrs. Bennet. Kate is sure Rebecca's active mind wanders as far away from Reverend Fleming's homily as hers.

"... am I not often inquiring, what shall I eat, what shall I drink, or wherewithal shall I be clothed? But the serious inquiry is, what shall I do to be saved?"

Saved, indeed.

The parishioners have been invited back to the rectory for tea. James sits in a corner playing spinning top with a few other children, while Mama visits with Mrs. Fleming and other ladies. Kate is happy that the Bennets are among those who stayed. Rebecca approaches Kate with a smile that would light a dark room. Holding out her hands, covered in white lace gloves, she takes Kate's hands.

"Dearest Kate. I've counted down the days to see you again, and you must know that attending church is never an event that I long for."

"Good to see you again." Kate feels her own hard shell beginning to crack open.

"I so wish Aunt and Uncle lived closer to town. I feel banished out in the hinterland. But perhaps that is the exact purpose."

"How much longer will you leave me in suspense?" Many scandalous scenarios have played through Kate's mind, but the only thing she is almost sure of is Rebecca's predicament must somehow involve a man.

"Not long now. But the Flemings' rectory is most definitely not the best place to tell you my tangled tale. Wait here." Rebecca walks over to her uncle, a round jolly man with a perpetually blotchy red face, and whispers something in his ear. At first, he shakes his head, gestures toward his wife. Rebecca's pleading brown eyes soon win him over. He finally smiles, shaking his head at how easily he was won over.

Rebecca approaches Kate with one hand held out flat,

circling a finger around the center of her palm. "I hold Uncle Raymond right here. He refuses me nothing. The carriage will be sent to your home to fetch me later. Come, show me one of your most secret sanctuaries in this town."

High clouds mute the sun. The winter air is crisp but without teeth.

"Will you tell me now?" Kate asks as they walk up a path toward Beacon Hill. A bald eagle and a red-tailed hawk both circle overhead, floating on a breeze, hunting for their next meal.

"Patience, dear Kate. I will explain all in due time, when we're even farther away from civilization." Rebecca glances up at the top of the hill. "What are those giant trees that stand like sentries?"

"Fir and cedar."

"Race you to them."

Rebecca picks up her skirt and starts up the path. Both laugh as they run through the long grass that is a lush green, now that the snow has melted. Rebecca stops suddenly and inspects the smallest of buds, ready to burst out of their winter covering on the alder trees. Kate passes her, runs as fast as her legs will take her, and reaches the top of the hill first. Rebecca soon follows and falls into Kate's arms, out of breath.

"I was distracted by the first sign of spring, which always makes me so hopeful," Rebecca says.

They stand in silence for a moment to catch their breath and watch a ship sailing away from Victoria on the Strait of Juan de Fuca. Snowy majestic peaks across the strait push through the skirt of clouds covering their base.

"Can you imagine a life sailing around the world to exotic places like Algiers, Greece, and Canton?" Rebecca says.

"Can you imagine being married to a naval officer?" Kate feels ashamed asking so blunt a question.

"Good God, no. Can you?"

"I have not really thought much about it." Kate knows she's a dreadful liar.

"I truly doubt that, Miss Katherine Harding. I saw you dance with Lieutenant Ashton at O'Brien's ball. It was clear you were both enamored of one another."

"But you danced the last waltz with him."

Rebecca laughs so hard she doubles over. "Dearest Kate, I have no designs on your officer. I am very much attracted to older rich men. It is not something I can help; it is just part of my lineage. My grandmother, mother, aunt, and my sister all married men much older and richer than they were."

They sit at the mossy base of Kate's favorite oak tree with the spidery branches. Her sanctuary.

"Tell me, does your scandal involve an older, richer man?"

"Older, richer, and ... married."

"Married?" Kate covers her mouth.

"But if only that were all the story involved. Shall I start from the beginning?"

Kate nods. A married man? She's now even more intrigued, and finds the most comfortable spot on the rock for what promises to be a long story.

"My father is a Wall Street merchant banker with Peabody, Morgan & Company. As long as I can remember, my mother has been a melancholic, sickly woman. I've heard she was not always this way, but I still have no idea what caused her to lose her vibrancy."

Kate has heard the same thing about *her* mama. That she somehow lost the exuberance she once had.

"Because of mother's disposition," Rebecca continues, "she never accompanied my father to business events or parties. When I turned sixteen, which was two years ago, it became my role to attend these functions with him."

"What kind of functions?"

"Private parties, dinners, balls, charity events—whenever the wealthy of Manhattan gathered. For business reasons, my father felt he needed to be there. It was at a small dinner party that I met Jeremiah Fortune."

"Fortune? Surely that can't be his real name."

"You're quite right. Jeremiah's surname is an affectation—mostly to make his mark among New York's business elite. 'Bogle' just didn't have the same impact. But what you need to know is that not only is Jeremiah a married man and fifteen years my senior, but he is also a Black man. Oh, dear Kate, I can tell by the look on your face that you are shocked, but please don't judge me."

"Of course, I won't judge you." But Kate *is* shocked. A married Black man? Could there be anything more scandalous? She imagines the moral outrage if she fell in love with a married man, let alone one who is a Black or a Chinaman or an Indian. Beyond forgiveness.

"Jeremiah was born in Saint Lucia, a small island in the Caribbean. Unlike the United States, where north and south are fighting a civil war at this very moment over the institution of slavery, it was abolished decades ago in Saint Lucia. Therefore, Jeremiah was born a free man. His family managed to build up a small empire in sugar cane, which led to his journey to the United States to invest the wealth. My father was the one he approached for investment advice."

Overhead, two crows cackle to one another, as if outraged by Rebecca's story.

"Is his wife with him in New York?"

Rebecca shakes her head. "She stayed back in Saint Lucia with no plans of joining him. The marriage was a financial arrangement between landowning families. According to Jeremiah, they have never loved one another or even consummated their marriage."

"When did you first meet him?"

"One year ago. I will never forget when he walked into the room, wearing a dark-blue tailored evening jacket with a jaunty red scarf. And then I was seated next to him at the dining-room table. It was clear not everyone was comfortable with him in attendance, but he and I spoke throughout dinner and the whole evening thereafter."

"What did you speak about?"

"Everything under the sun. Poetry, philosophy, politics ... He is highly intelligent and very well read. And his smile ..." Rebecca looks off to the mountains across the strait. "After that evening, I knew Plato's story of soul mates to be true."

"Soul mates?"

"Have you not read Plato's *Symposium*? The story reads something like this: Long ago, all people had four arms, four legs, a head with two faces, and one soul. Fearing their power, Zeus, the god of sky and thunder, split everyone into two. Therefore, according to Plato, people spend their whole lives desperate to reunite with the other half of their soul. I have never been more sure of anything in my life than that Jeremiah is my soul mate."

Kate wonders if Hugh is hers. Their first meeting on the street, and the few times since, sent electricity throughout her body. But does that mean anything? She can't say she even knows him.

"How did your association evolve?" Kate asks.

"Our paths crossed when I attended more business events with my father. We then met for secret lunches, walks in Central Park, dinners. But you must know, Kate, there has been no impropriety beyond our clandestine meetings. Yes, we have been alone together—which is a scandal in and of itself—but nothing untoward has happened, other than both of us falling hopelessly and madly in love with one another."

"How were you found out?"

"A business associate of my father's saw us out together. We may have been holding hands. Jeremiah may have kissed me." Rebecca looks at Kate sheepishly, as if she's expecting a reproachful look.

"And then your parents sent you away to the British Colony of Vancouver Island, on the opposite side of the continent from the man you love."

"Precisely. Tell me you don't think unkindly toward me, Kate."

"Never would I. Have you written to or received any letters from Mr. Fortune since you've been in Victoria?"

"I have secretly sent a few letters, but I'm sure my aunt and uncle have strict instructions from my father to intercept any mail sent to me from Jeremiah."

"He could send his letters to me at my address. I will pass them on to you." The thought of facilitating Rebecca's connection with Jeremiah Fortune floods Kate with a guilty exhilaration.

Rebecca's large brown eyes open wide. "You would do that for me?"

"Yes, of course."

"My true and dear friend." Rebecca throws her arms around Kate and holds her for several moments.

In front of Kate's house, a coachman stands at the door of the carriage, as Kate and Rebecca say their goodbyes.

"I'm dreadfully sorry that I monopolized our whole conversation today, but you were such a willing and welcome ear," Rebecca says.

"I am happy to listen."

"You are such a dear friend. Next time, I want to hear all about your life, in microscopic detail."

"I am afraid it will be a very short exchange."

"You have such a curious nature, and I know you must have secret dreams to share, at the very least."

Kate smiles and nods. But what good are dreams, really, when they seem impossible to fulfill?

Rebecca gives Kate a hug and a quick peck on the cheek. The coachman offers Rebecca his hand as she climbs into the carriage. As the carriage makes its way down the long drive, through the trees Kate sees large billowing sails being hoisted on a ship in the harbor. She is sure it is the HMS *Forward*. And it's heading back out to sea.

Lucy places bowls of soup and a plate of bread on the dining room table, where only Kate and Papa sit for dinner. Mama went to her room soon after church, claiming she had a headache, and asked for her dinner to be brought to her. Kate is sure the headache has everything to do with Arthur's letter.

"Papa, you have such a grave expression, as if something very heavy is weighing on you. Did you have a difficult day at Craigflower Farm?"

Papa shakes his head and picks up a piece of bread and a butter knife. "It is nothing to concern you, Kitty."

"Is it Arthur's letter that's causing you such grief?"

"If only that were all." He finishes buttering his bread and takes a bite.

"What is it, Papa? You can tell me. I am old enough to hear your news."

Papa doesn't answer. He spoons a mouthful of soup.

"Is it our family's financial predicament?"

"I cannot speak of this to you, Kitty. It is my responsibility alone, and I do not wish to hear another word from you on this subject."

He never speaks to her in such a harsh tone. Perhaps an overseas creditor has called in a loan?

"Might we lose our house?"

Papa looks up at Kate. Obviously, she has hit a nerve. Their family home is in jeopardy. She has lost her appetite and can only stare into her bowl. Why is he so stubborn? Although a teaching job at St. Ann's would not bring in vast sums of money, it would help. But Kate knows that, ultimately, it will not be Papa's responsibility alone. She will be forced to marry Eamonn O'Brien, who will pay off all the Harding debts and set up the family nicely for the future. A shiver of hopelessness washes over her.

"I did receive some good news today," Papa says, quickly changing the subject. "Captain Lascelles from the HMS *Forward* has offered to host an event on the ship to raise money to build the new hospital. Apparently, some of the crew will be entertaining with songs and plays. And there will be dancing, of course."

"On the HMS *Forward*?" Kate tries to temper her voice so as not to show too much excitement. "Is that right? When will this be?"

"Friday, February fourteenth."

"St. Valentine's Day?"

"Yes. It was thought a theme would appeal to the community and draw more people out."

The chance to see Hugh Ashton on Valentine's Day most definitely appeals to her. She can't wait to tell Rebecca.

# Chapter 12

Kate is free to perform her clandestine research in the surgery without fear of being caught. Papa hitched up the carriage early this morning to do his rounds, tending to the Lidgates, McPhails, and other settlers in Saanich. And Mama, although still stubbornly mourning, and holed up in her room most days, agreed to keep him company on the journey up the peninsula.

Outside the window, billowing dark clouds churn on the horizon, promising a downpour. The rain will most likely reach all the way to Saanich. Kate thinks Lucy is optimistic, as she struggles with a forceful wind to hang clean bed linen on the clothesline to dry.

Kate pulls out dusty bottles from the medicine chest she hasn't yet recorded. She then searches for entries in Papa's notebooks to explain how the potions remedy particular illnesses, and writes everything down in her own notes.

*Squill—stimulates bronchial mucous membrane ... diuretic, emetic and expectorant ... lowers the pulse ... most useful in Dropsy ...*

*Silver—A sedative tonic in relieving morbid irritability ...*

She guiltily considers whether Mama's tea needs to be laced with silver to relieve her morbid irritability. Has Papa ever thought the same?

Out the window, Lucy speaks to a tall thin man, oily hair slicked to his head, and wearing a tattered topcoat and muddy trousers. He helps a woman step down from what looks like a vegetable cart. Her woolen coat is equally as dirty and ragged. Kate almost drops a bottle when the woman's scream pierces the silence. The man scoops the woman in his arms, and Kate meets them at the surgery door, where Lucy has led them.

"Pleeze 'elp wive." the man says in a thick accent. The woman, with long black hair and a dark complexion, looks childlike draped over his arms. She moans against his neck.

"My papa ... the doctor isn't here." Kate says. "You see, there's no one here to help you." She sweeps her arms around the empty room, trying to get her point across. "There are other doctors in Victoria. Perhaps you could try Dr. Helmcken."

The man's face looks blank—he obviously doesn't understand English. The woman again cries out in pain. The man takes off the woman's coat to reveal a swollen pregnant belly.

Kate and Lucy share an anxious look.

"You need a midwife, sir," Kate says.

"I'll boil water," Lucy says and turns toward the door.

"But, Lucy, we can't." Panic rises up inside Kate. "Put the water on and then quickly fetch Lady Douglas."

Lucy nods and rushes out of the room, while Kate removes a stack of sheets from the cupboard and covers the examining table. The man's dark green eyes are pleading, as he helps his wife onto the table. While he comforts his wife, who moans in agony, Kate lifts up the woman's dress. No blood. Thank the heavens for that. But the dress is soaked. Her waters must have broken. Kate puts her hands on the woman's belly like Lady Douglas did with Mama, but she's not sure what information she's supposed to glean from doing so. She only feels the muscles tighten in contractions as the woman moans and thrashes in pain. Feeling utterly helpless, Kate wets a cloth and wipes the woman's hot, sweaty face. The woman looks at her with terrified eyes.

"Agata," the man says, pointing to his wife. "Tomasz," he says and points to himself.

"I am Kate."

"*Polska*."

"Ah, Polish. Are you here because of gold?"

He nods. "*Tak*. Gold."

Outside, the skies open up and rain pours down.

After several minutes, Lucy enters the surgery, hair and clothing dripping wet, with a pile of towels over her shoulder and carrying a large bucket of steaming water.

"Lady Douglas is away. Not in Victoria," Lucy says.

The man stands and takes the heavy load from Lucy, while she places the towels on a side table.

"What are we to do, Lucy?" Kate says. Dread snakes its way through her body.

"Help the baby come out," Lucy says, matter of fact.

"But how?"

Lucy begins taking off the woman's dress as if assisting at a birth is an everyday occurrence for her. Maybe it is on the reserve. Kate helps Lucy pull the damp light cotton dress over Agata's head, definitely not warm enough for the west coast winter. She wears no corset, only a petticoat and pantaloons. While Lucy helps Agata off with the wet pantaloons, Kate rummages around the drawers in a large bureau to find soap. After she lathers her hands and up her arms as Lady Douglas taught her, she hands the soap to Lucy, who follows suit.

Lucy gently helps Agata bend her knees and splay her legs. Agata's body curls in another agonizing contraction. She screams out, moans in Polish. Tomasz strokes her hair, speaks comforting words to her.

Kate goes to the bottom of the examining table and pulls up Agata's petticoat. Breathes deeply several times to calm her jagged nerves. When Lady Douglas delivered baby Violet, she felt for the position of the head. Kate touches a soft mound.

"I feel the baby's head," Kate says to Lucy. "Do you know what to do?"

Lucy shakes her head. Agata's screams become fiercer. The rain is now hammering at the windows, blurring the view of the field and barn. Kate nervously scrubs her hands again, rifles through the medicine chest, and finds a bottle of chloroform. She opens the bottle, places several drops in a cloth and puts it near Agata's face.

"Hold it here, a little way from her face, for her to breathe in," she says to Lucy.

Soon Agata is calmer, moaning quietly. But even with all the tortuous contractions, the baby has barely moved in the birth canal. If the baby remains stuck, both mother and child will die. Kate opens the chest of medical instruments and finds forceps the shape of large salad spoons, hinged at the end. She remembers reading about the use of forceps in childbirth, but cannot recall in which of Papa's medical textbooks. She scans the bookshelf, but knows there is no time to search. Tomasz looks frightened, as she slowly and carefully guides the instrument into Agata's now limp body. With a hand on Agata's belly, and when she feels it harden with a contraction, she slowly pulls on the forceps. Blood appears. Did she do something wrong? Kate looks up at Lucy.

"No worry," Lucy says, nodding for her to keep going.

It takes several more contractions and gentle tugs before the head and torso are exposed. Not long after, the baby slides out onto the table.

"It's a boy," Kate says.

Lucy's smile gives Kate some badly needed courage. Tomasz covers his mouth, tears streaming down his face. He speaks to an almost unconscious Agata. Strokes her hair, kisses her forehead. But the baby is blue and lifeless. The cord is firmly wrapped around his neck. Kate freezes. She's paralyzed. Lucy quickly steps in and unwraps the cord. The limp body doesn't move. Lucy cleans out the baby's mouth with her finger. Picks up the limp body and rubs its chest and back. Soon he spouts out a weak cry. Oh, thank God.

After Kate uses a scissor-like instrument to sever the umbilical cord, Lucy cleans and wraps the baby boy in a towel and hands him to his mother.

Agata and Tomasz, both in tears, repeat, "Dziękuję ci ... thank you," over and over, as they admire their new son. It suddenly dawns on Kate that both mother and baby could easily have died in her hands, and she feels lightheaded. Is this what Papa faces on a daily basis? Treating patients whose life and death rest in the balance? This thought both terrifies and excites her beyond all measure.

The rain has stopped, but the air is laden with a thick mist. Lucy makes a bed of blankets and straw in the back of the cart for Agata and the baby.

Tomasz pulls a few coins out of his pocket and hands them to Kate. She shakes her head.

"No need. Just take care of your family," Kate says.

Tomasz nods and puts his hand over his heart in appreciation. He then picks up the wooden handles in the front.

Kate wraps a surprised Lucy in a hug, says, "I could not

have done this without you, Lucy." Tiny baby cries echo off the trees, as the cart heads back down the muddy road.

Horses and carriages splash through deep puddles on Government Street.

"I did only what any midwife would have done," Kate says, as she and Sister Mary Providence make their way down the plank walkway. "Not exactly what I would call a medical procedure."

"Do not diminish your accomplishment, Katherine. You may have saved the lives of both mother and child. You had the knowledge and forethought to use chloroform to sedate the woman, and you used forceps to aid the birth. It sounds exactly like what a physician would do."

Women smile and nod, and men tip their hats as they pass. "Thanks to Papa's medical textbooks and notes. But it was Lucy who saved the baby boy's life. She knew to unwrap the cord and bring him to life."

"Something to learn from her." When they cross Yates Street, Sister Mary's heavy black cloak swishes in the mud. "Did I mention to you that Elizabeth Blackwell studied obstetrics at the famed Parisian maternity hospital, *La Maternité*, and was acclaimed by her teachers as a superb obstetrician? Perhaps you will follow in her footsteps, one day."

From Kate's own family experience, she knows how perilous life can be for both mother and infant during childbirth. It seems more babies die at birth than survive to adulthood.

"Midwives have assisted women in childbirth since the beginning of time. I am curious when obstetrics became a profession."

"I believe it was in the last century when male barber-surgeons, who were trained by physicians to assist midwives during difficult births, refused to pass down their knowledge."

Perhaps it's right that the medical profession intervened. Kate has read that women are at a high risk of losing their own lives from hemorrhage, during or after the birth, or contracting puerperal pyrexia infection. Figuring out how to prevent these threats does interest Kate a great deal. Perhaps she *will* study obstetrics one day. Can she even venture to dream about this? Sister Mary seems more confident about her future than she is.

When they reach St. Ann's School, Lucy is at the door, helping James button up his coat.

"Oh, Lucy, you are here. Did I forget to tell you I would walk James home today?" Kate says.

"I did washing, went to shops, and plucked a chicken for dinner."

"All of that, after helping deliver a baby this morning," Sister Mary says.

"Miss Kate did most of the work," Lucy says, tightening James's shoelace.

"That is not true, Lucy," Kate says. "Mother and child would have been in peril without your help."

She scrutinizes Lucy's thick, tarnished chain necklace with a large turquoise medallion, and large silver earrings, like tiny chandeliers that dangle almost to her shoulders. Lucy is far from timid about wearing mismatched and entirely inappropriate jewelry. Kate can't imagine how these garish adornments will add to her dowry, but Lucy is certain they will.

"I like it better when Lucy walks me home," James says with a pout. "She lets me splash in puddles and dawdle. You do not like it when I dawdle, Kate. And Lucy tells me stories."

Sister Mary and Kate share a smile.

"Will you at least allow me to walk with you and Lucy?" Kate asks.

"I suppose." But James doesn't sound happy about it.

Walking ahead of Kate, James firmly holds Lucy's hand, as they make their way down Broad Street. The rain begins again. Kate looks up at the gray sky, closes her eyes, lets the small drops tickle her face. The first calm moment in her day.

"Look, a raven!" James says excitedly, pointing to the sky.

"Crow. A raven much bigger," Lucy says.

"Tell me again about the raven."

"I told you many times." Lucy smiles at James.

"Again, please, Lucy."

"Raven is one of the Creators—discovered man in a clamshell. He brings fire to people, and he can change his shape to animal or human."

"You forgot the part about the light."

"Yes, Raven freed the light."

"From boxes inside boxes inside boxes made of cedar, that an old man and his daughter kept from people," he says.

Lucy nods.

James continues, "Raven stole the sun from the old man but tripped, and the moon and stars were chipped off the sun's light and now sit in the night sky."

Kate can't help but think James is much more interested in Lucy's stories than ones from the Bible he hears at church, or ones that Mama reads to him.

"Now I tell the story of *Tzunequa*, wild woman of the woods," Lucy says. "If you not listen to your Mama or Papa and return home before dark, she will chase and eat you."

Lucy chases James; he runs away from her, squealing with laughter. Lucy stops just before the bridge, picks up James, and swings him around. Although he is becoming too big to do so, he wraps his legs around Lucy's hips and rests his head on her shoulder. She kisses his forehead and carries him across the bridge. A longing bubbles up from deep inside of Kate. She can't recall ever receiving that same love and attention. From anyone.

Kate and her parents sit at the dining room table, while Lucy carries in plates of food.

"I must say, Kitty, I am quite impressed," Papa says as he carves a chicken. "Delivering a baby. Well done."

"Could you not have called on Lady Douglas or Dr. Helmcken?" Mama says, looking less impressed, as she takes a plate of steaming vegetables from Lucy.

"There was no time, Mama. The labor was in an advanced stage."

"I will be sure to seek out this couple and check on the mother and infant," Papa says.

"I could not have delivered the baby without Lucy's help," Kate says. "She is the one who saved the wee boy."

"Is that right?" Mama says, softening.

"Well done, Lucy," Papa says.

Lucy and Kate share a smile.

"And, Lucy, I ... well ... I've been meaning to tell you ..." Mama stumbles on her words. "James is very happy in your care. We wish to thank you for your service."

Mama has finally acknowledged Lucy's value. And directly to her. Something has changed.

Lucy nods and leaves the dining room.

# Chapter 13

"Oh, my dearest Kate," Rebecca says, leaning forward, her inner eyebrows pinched in sympathy. Dull sun casts little light and no warmth, as she and Kate sit on either end of the window seat in the Bennets' sitting room. "You carry around your hopes and dreams like a heavy packsack."

There's a knock on the door, and Han, the houseboy, carries in a tray of tea and biscuits. He pours tea into delicate china cups, painted with bright red roses, and places the tea and the biscuits on a table in front of them. Rebecca thanks him. He bows and exits the room. So polished and professional compared to the string of housemaids hired by the Harding household. But Kate is almost sure Han doesn't provide the Bennets with delicious clams, crab, salmon, and halibut fresh from the ocean.

"Why could I not have been born a boy, instead of a girl who has so few options in life?" Kate looks out the window at the bare fields that stretch right to the ocean. "If my brother and I reversed our genders, he could be painting to his heart's content—an acceptable vocation for a woman—and I could be at St. George's studying medicine."

"But you have such a strong mind, formidable intellect, and an independent spirit. You remind me of Jane Eyre."

"Who is she?"

Rebecca goes to a bookshelf, pulls out a novel, and shows the cover to Kate. *Jane Eyre* by Charlotte Bronte.

"It's yours; a gift from me. You must read this book, if only to take solace that there is another female, albeit a fictional one, who shares your struggling spirit. This novel stirred much controversy when it was published, which made it absolutely delicious to read!"

"What kind of controversy?"

"It challenges notions of religion, morality, and women's place in society. The book was first published under the name Currer Bell as a *nom de plume*—it was thought no one would read such a book if it was written by a woman. I must read a passage that will resonate deeply. This is where Jane Eyre argues with Mr. Rochester, a dark and impassioned man, who owns the estate where she is governess. That is all I will tell you, so as not to ruin the story for you."

Rebecca flips through the pages.

"Ah, here it is.

> *"'Jane, be still; don't struggle so, like a wild frantic bird that is rending its own plumage in its desperation.'*
>
> *"'I am no bird; and no net ensnares me; I am a free human being with an independent will, which I now exert to leave you.'"*

Rebecca looks up for a reaction.

"Most of the time I do struggle like a wild bird thrashing in a net," Kate says.

"But don't you see? You are also a free human being with an independent will. I just know that, in time, you will somehow find your way, dear Kate."

A free human being with an independent will. Kate takes the book from Rebecca and reads the passage over and over. Are there women in society who truly feel this power of freedom and independence? If so, Elizabeth Blackwell must be one of them.

"And what about you? Is your dream to marry Jeremiah Fortune?"

"Yes, but we have all of society against us. I am not sure if our battle to be husband and wife will ever be won, but I'm not willing to give up hope just yet. Perhaps we could live blissfully on some remote Caribbean island, away from the harsh judgment."

"Will your parents try to force another suitor on you, as my mama is forcing Mr. O'Brien onto me?"

"I'm sure there will be men lined up upon my return to New York City. But I will not accept any of them. I would rather die a wrinkled old spinster before I marry a man I do not love."

Kate feels exactly the same way about marrying Eamonn O'Brien. But would she allow her family to fall into financial ruin, when she could be their savior, by accepting a proposal from this wealthy man? Thinking about this conundrum makes her lightheaded.

The Bennets' coachman waits by the open carriage door, as Kate and Rebecca say their goodbyes.

"I'll see you in just a few days' time at the St. Valentine's party," Kate says.

"Aboard the HMS *Forward*, no less. Your eyes just lit up, dear Kate. You must be thinking of Lieutenant Hugh Ashton right this very moment."

"Perhaps." Kate feels a flush come over her face. She hasn't seen Hugh for over a month, since they crossed paths on the beach. She wonders if he has thought of her as much as she has thought of him, during this time. If he has even thought of her at all.

"I look forward to hearing your review." Rebecca gestures to the novel in Kate's hand. "I'm sure the character of Jane Eyre will be like a mirror into your own soul."

Kate smiles at Rebecca—never before has she met someone with such romantic notions.

"I am very sad for you, but so overjoyed for me that your parents sent you to Vancouver Island." Kate hugs Rebecca tightly, and the coachman helps her into the carriage. As the carriage sets off, Kate looks out the back window and waves goodbye to Rebecca.

When the carriage makes its way down the drive to the Harding home, Kate sees Papa standing at the front door, supervising workmen, who load the antique dining room buffet into a large covered wagon, pulled by mammoth Clydesdale horses. The buffet was shipped over from England, when they moved halfway across the world; it has been in the Harding family for generations.

"Papa, what is happening?"

The grave look on his face tells Kate he'd rather not discuss it. Especially with her.

"Judge Begbie has purchased these pieces."

"Are we in such dire financial straits that we are now forced to sell off our furniture?"

His body begins to shake. Anger and frustration explode out of the finger he points at her as he speaks. She has never seen him in such a state.

"Don't you believe for one moment that any amount of teaching work at St. Ann's School will make even a slight difference to our financial fortunes."

Kate follows as he storms into the house. "But, Papa ..."

"Enough!" His feet pound on the wooden floor all the way to the surgery.

In the front hallway are the delicately carved dresser from the spare room upstairs and two Indonesian teak side tables. The two burly workers enter the front door, lift the heavy dresser, and head down the front steps to load it into the wagon.

Lucy appears from the kitchen, looking distraught because of the commotion. "Mrs. Harding locked in her room again. Won't take tea."

Kate puts her hand on Lucy's arm. "Nothing for you to worry about, Lucy. Mama likes to be alone sometimes, that is all."

But Kate can only imagine the state Mama is in. The humiliation of having to sell off family heirlooms, in order to pay household bills, will be too much for her to bear. Will it be enough to pay off debts, or will they still lose their home? An image flashes through Kate's mind of her in a wedding dress, walking down the church aisle toward Mr. O'Brien. She vigorously shakes her head to chase it away, as the workmen walk back through the door to take the two remaining tables.

Kate watches the loaded wagon bump down the drive, then closes the front door. She peers into the dining room and sees the empty space where the large buffet used to hold the china and silverware, which are now packed away in wooden crates. She slumps up the stairs to her room. On the desk is a letter from Arthur. If only he knew the extent of the trauma their family was going through. But he's going through his own kind of hell. She rips open the envelope.

*London*

*2 Nov '61*

*My dearest Kate,*

*It feels like an eternity since I have heard from you. I hope you are not angry with me, as I could not bear the thought. I can only imagine how shocked and distressed Mama and Papa must be with my new life. Change has never come easily for Mama, and I'm sure Papa is deeply disappointed in me. But there is nothing that can be undone now.*

*I am cobbling together a living in London's East End as an apprentice cabinetmaker with Mr. Morgan, a short, thickset man whose manner is as rough as the skin on his hands. His red nose sits to one side of his wide face like a plump sausage, and he has more teeth missing than are still attached to his gums. Because of the added space in his mouth, spittle sprays out whenever he speaks, which is much too often, in my opinion. But although his craftsmanship is a far cry from Thomas Sheraton's neoclassical marvels, I have come to admire Morgan's choice of exotic woods and his exaggerated curves and decorative carvings. I am currently working on an exquisite rosewood dining table, of which I am quite proud.*

*Morgan's eighteen-year-old daughter Rachel—a surprisingly pretty girl with hair the colour of mahogany—has made it clear she has eyes for me. This attention is new and somewhat unsettling for me. Other than a brief flirtation with Charlotte Atwood, the girl I met at Uncle Charles and Aunt Adelaide's annual summer garden party a few years ago, I have had no romantic encounters. A sad state of affairs, to be sure, that I feel pleased by the attentions of a workingman's daughter.*

*Still, my dream is to live in Paris among artists as determined as I to make painting a vocation. I have downgraded my living quarters at the rooming house where I am staying, which will save me several shillings per month. I now sleep in a room with five factory workers, who reek of coal and sweat and bathe very infrequently. However, these coarse men make for interesting subjects to sketch. I have included a sample for you in this letter.*

*I must sign off now. I think of you often, dear sister.*

*Yours,*

*Arthur*

On the following page are sketches of the five men Arthur described. He has represented not only their physical appearance but also something deep and profound in their faces. As if their weary souls are seeping right through the ink. He must nurture this talent at all costs.

Kate flops on her bed, opens the thick hard cover of *Jane Eyre*, and begins reading from the beginning.

*There was no possibility of taking a walk that day ...*

After a few paragraphs, she stops reading, and instead flips to the passage that Rebecca marked for her.

*"Jane, be still; don't struggle so, like a wild frantic bird that is rending its own plumage in its desperation."*

*"I am no bird; and no net ensnares me; I*

*am a free human being with an independent will, which I now exert to leave you."*

Kate puts down the book and lies back. She rests her head on the pillow, imagines herself trapped in a cage, kicking and flailing her limbs.

# Chapter 14

Lively music plays, as Kate and her parents walk up the gangplank to board the HMS *Forward*. People are milling about the ship's deck that is lit with oil lanterns. The three giant masts, hundreds of feet tall, loom over the festivities. Like Kate, most women wear red dresses for the Valentine's Day occasion. Mama had one of her gowns re-tailored for Kate—crimson silk, finished with fine white lace around the neck and waist, and scalloped at the bottom. Mama also lent Kate a delicate string of pearls with teardrop earrings to match, which Lucy greatly admired. Even Mama's velvet gown looks to be more a shade of deep burgundy than black, although there are still many more months of mourning ahead.

Through open doors, Kate sees the ship's orchestral ensemble playing on a small stage at one end of a large room. Hugh is not among them. Does he even play an instrument? She doesn't know. In fact, she knows very little about Lieutenant Ashton. Officers, who look their finest in clean and pressed blue uniforms, greet the guests as they arrive, including Mr. and Mrs. Trutch, Governor Douglas, Mr. and Mrs. Work, and Judge Begbie. Kate's stomach sours when she sees Mr. O'Brien from across the deck. He sent her an impossibly large bouquet of Valentine's Day flowers this morning. O'Brien's bright red vest doesn't nearly cover his rotund belly. He smokes an enormous cigar, surely boring the crewmen circled around him with his embellished tales.

Hugh is nowhere to be seen. Perhaps he is one of the performers preparing behind the stage.

Fanny and Emily wave to Kate from across the deck. Both stand out from the guests in their own way, wearing dull dusty pink (Fanny) and outrageous tangerine orange (Emily). Poor Henry and Philip are once again captives in their company.

Kate and her parents make their way into the large dining hall, decorated with red paper hearts, red ribbons, and red and white streamers hanging from the tall ceiling. Sailors in bleached white uniforms with blue collars and cuffs carry around trays of drinks. A vase of white carnations sits in the middle of each red-linen-covered table. Guests begin lining up at the back of the room, at long tables filled with cold meats, fish, cheeses and bread, fancy petit fours, and heart-shaped cakes.

Rebecca is seated at a table, entertaining Mr. Connelly, the banker, who was so obviously taken with her at O'Brien's ball. Connelly's laugh is heard from across the room. When Rebecca spots Kate, she excuses herself from the table and hurries over.

"You look simply divine, Miss Katherine Harding," she says, holding Kate's hands and pecking her cheek. "Lieutenant Ashton will be spellbound, I am sure of it."

"And look at you. I have never seen fabric quite so exquisite." Rebecca's cranberry gown rests off her shoulders and shimmers in the light.

"My papa takes pride in dressing his daughter in the most expensive of clothing and adornments. He is rather extravagant, I must say. But I will be the last to complain."

A large bell, one that probably calls the ship's crew for meals, rings so loudly Kate feels it vibrate not only in her ears but also her chest. The ship's Captain Lascelles walks onto the stage.

"Welcome aboard HMS *Forward*. We are so very pleased to be able to give something back to the people of Victoria, who have so eagerly embraced both officers and crew."

Rebecca whispers in Kate's ear, "I will bet you cannot wait to embrace one officer in particular."

Kate smiles and playfully nudges her.

"I am pleased to tell you that we have already raised several thousand dollars for the new hospital fund, thanks to you and to generous donors such as Mr. Eamonn O'Brien."

Cheers and claps from the audience. O'Brien puffs up his chest. He scans the crowd and rests his self-important gaze on Kate. Does he care even a whit about a new hospital? Or has he only donated his sum to impress Papa to win her hand?

Captain Lascelles continues, "The officers and crew have worked tirelessly to put together a special night of theatrics, poetry, and song for this St. Valentine's Day. Please find a seat, as we are ready to begin."

Kate sees O'Brien move in her direction, so she takes Rebecca by the hand and leads her to a table right near the front.

The entertainment begins with a love ballad, "All Things Love Thee, So Do I," sung by a tall, thin, balding officer with a beautiful voice.

*Gentle waves upon the deep,*
*Murmur soft when thou dost sleep,*
*Little birds upon the tree,*

*Sing their sweetest songs for thee,*
*their sweetest songs for thee.*

O'Brien catches Kate's eye. He leers at her, stroking his moustache, which makes Kate's stomach churn. During the song's chorus, the only one she can think about is Hugh.

*All things love thee, so do I,*
*When thou dost in slumbers lie,*
*All things love thee, so do I*

After the ballad is a pantomime comedy play, in which a hopeful lover tries to woo his sweetheart by playing a guitar and humming a song—both very badly—while a long line of dapper suitors distracts "her." The sweetheart's white gown is decorated with red hearts, including one placed on each of the rubber-ball-filled bosoms. In place of dialogue, the band makes comical sounds to accompany the exaggerated gestures of the actors. Kate laughs at the crazy antics. At first, she wonders if the man playing the sweetheart could be Hugh, disguised in a pink wig, with a thick coat of makeup, including turquoise painted above the eyes and bright red circles on his cheeks. She quickly decides not.

The next act is a group of sailors wearing long white stretchy-cotton trousers and sleeveless shirts that look like undergarments, which makes Kate feel both excited and a bit ashamed, as she gapes at the broad chests and shoulders, muscular arms, and handsome faces. The tumbles and rolls, headstands and handstands demonstrate their strength and balance in gymnastics. But the finale is stunning when four men bear the weight of a small wooden platform on their shoulders. Two men stand on the platform and two more climb atop the first men's shoulders and balance, creating a human pyramid. They dismount with skill and grace Kate didn't know men could possess.

Everyone is still clapping for the gymnasts when Hugh walks onto the stage. Kate involuntarily gasps and covers her mouth. Rebecca slips her arm in Kate's and glances at her with a big smile. Hugh, looking even more handsome in his uniform, his brown wavy hair neatly combed back, peers out into the audience, looking around the entire room. When he sets his eyes on Kate, his search stops. He smiles and nods at her. Her heart trips several beats.

"In honor of St. Valentine's Day, I would like to recite a poem by perhaps one of the most flamboyant and notorious of the Romantic poets, and one of my own personal favorites,

Lord Byron. I would like to dedicate this poem to a young lassie with whom I have recently become acquainted here in Victoria."

Rebecca nudges Kate. Is she the young lassie he speaks of, or has he met someone else? There's no way to be sure, since she has hardly seen him the last while. But when he begins reciting the poem by heart, his eyes barely leave hers. She must be the one.

*She walks in beauty, like the night*
*Of cloudless clime and starry skies;*
*And all that's best of dark and bright*
*Meet her aspect and her eyes ...*

Kate is completely and totally mesmerized by Hugh, as he recites the poem to great effect, with perfect inflection and cadence. He could easily do justice to Shakespeare's words on the stage, acting King Lear, Macbeth, or Hamlet.

*... One shade the more, one ray the less*
*Had half impaired the nameless grace*
*Which waves in every raven tress ...*

Hugh lingers on this last line, eyes still on Kate. People are sure to know who the lassie with the raven tresses is. Kate looks over at O'Brien, whose hand that was stroking his moustache is now a fist. His forehead is creased in anger. She is distracted from Hugh's recitation and can feel Mama's penetrating stare from behind pierce into her spine.

*... But tell of days in goodness spent*
*A mind at peace with all below,*
*A heart whose love is innocent.*

Hugh receives enthusiastic applause as he bows.

"That is all the entertainment for you this evening, ladies and gentlemen," he says. "Please help yourself to more food and drinks. The room will soon be cleared of tables, to make way for the dance that will end the evening."

His gaze once more lingers on Kate before he leaves the stage.

"It was as if only the two of you existed in the entire world," Rebecca says.

"You don't think anyone else noticed, do you?"

"Only those who are blind and have no heart."

Mama weaves quickly through the crowd, heading right for

Kate. O'Brien is coming toward her from the other direction. Hugh is talking with his fellow officers in front of the stage.

"Go, quickly," Rebecca says, gesturing to Hugh.

Kate weaves through the guests and reaches Hugh.

"Would you be so kind as to take me on a tour of this fine ship, Lieutenant Ashton?"

"It would be my pleasure, Miss Harding," Hugh says with a delighted smile. The young officers nudge Hugh teasingly and bow to Kate.

She turns to see both O'Brien and Mama closing in, so she links her arm in Hugh's and pulls him toward the door by the stage.

"You seem in a dreadful hurry. I didn't know you were so interested in naval vessels."

"Ships travel in and out of Victoria's harbor daily, and I have yet to see the workings from the inside." Kate glances over her shoulder. Neither O'Brien nor Mama is following.

Hugh takes her by the hand. "Come with me, then."

They exit a side door by the stage and down a staircase. Kate releases his hand and walks through the long area below, lined with several guns—cannons that fire explosive projectiles. There's an acrid and sour smell that is most likely spent gunpowder.

"As you can see, we are on the upper gun deck." Hugh speaks formally as he starts his tour.

Kate takes a closer look at the cannons, imagines their formidable destructive power. Touches the cold metal.

Hugh continues, "There are twelve guns altogether, each weighing over two tonnes ..."

Kate recalls learning from Papa that in 1850, a warship like this bombarded the Kwakiutl village on northern Vancouver Island, in retaliation for settlers being killed.

"This ship carries several tonnes of armament. And the—"

"Do you believe it is just, to destroy native villages with this much power and might?" Kate asks.

"It is the duty of the British Navy to protect the land and people, and enforce colonial law and order. When natives loot our ships and kill our settlers, there must be a forceful response."

"But surely they are only trying to protect *their* land and people. There must be ways to enforce colonial order other than military might."

Hugh walks over to her. Cups his hand gently on her cheek.

"My dear Kate. Not only do you have a prodigious intellect, but also a very soft heart."

He stands so close she can feel his warm breath.

"Am I the one? The lassie you dedicated the poem to?"

"What do you think?"

Kate moves away from him. "I cannot be certain. Our paths have not crossed for weeks. Perhaps you have met other young women in this town."

"Victoria isn't exactly overflowing with young women. By my estimate, there are at least fifty men for every woman."

"It's at least double that number."

"You say there are approximately one hundred men for every woman? How could I be so fortunate to be alone, on the gun deck of the HMS *Forward*, with the most vivacious, eccentric, and beautiful woman of them all?"

Hugh steps close again and looks deeply into her eyes. He takes her face in his hands and presses his lips to hers. A new and surprising quiver of excitement pulses through her body, from her lips to her toes and back again. Other intense sensations overcome her: the warmth and softness of his lips; his breath that smells of sweet wine; the heat of her body; the prickle of the stubble on his chin; the intense pleasure around her mouth, in her chest, deep inside her body. Voices are heard at the top of the stairs. Hugh and Kate quickly disengage. Both are flushed as an officer descends the stairs with guests.

"There is also a middle- and lower-gun deck," the officer says. "Oh, I see the Drisdales are not the only Victorians interested in our ship." By the look on his face and the tone in his voice, it's clear Kate and Hugh haven't fooled anyone.

"Yes, sir," Hugh says and leads Kate to the stairway. "As I was saying, the two-cylinder horizontal single-expansion direct-acting steam engines can power this ship up to a speed of over seven knots."

"Is that so?" Kate says, following Hugh up the stairs.

When they get to the top deck, they both burst out laughing. The orchestra is warming up in the dining hall.

"Best if we enter separately," Kate says.

Hugh looks around to make sure no one is watching, and gives Kate another deep kiss before she opens the door.

Tables and chairs have been cleared to make way for a large dance floor. She touches her lips, still feels the tingle of Hugh's kiss. Mr. Connelly looks as if he's under Rebecca's spell, as he adoringly watches her every gesture and movement, while she charms him with another of her stories. Mama is chatting with a group at the back of the room, but O'Brien is nowhere to be seen. Could he have left so soon? Is it possible she will enjoy the remainder of the evening without O'Brien insinuating himself upon her? Papa climbs onto the stage and the guests grow quiet.

"Good evening, ladies and gentlemen. My name is Dr. William Harding and, as many of you know, I was one of the first doctors who came from England to serve the Hudson's Bay Company at Fort Victoria. That was over seven years ago now. The fort will soon be dismantled, as our town has increased in numbers over the past years."

Kate looks around the room. She is filled with pride at the looks of respect and admiration for Papa.

"A new medical facility is vital to properly care for the residents. As the doctor overseeing the building of Victoria's new hospital, I want to thank each and every one of you for supporting this worthy cause. But I would like to extend my most heartfelt gratitude to Captain Lascelles and the officers and crew of the HMS *Forward* for so generously donating their resources, time—and as we witnessed earlier, their talents—for the benefit of our community. The orchestra is now ready. Let the dancing begin."

As the guests clap for Papa, the orchestra begins playing a schottische and everyone flocks to the dance floor, including Papa and Mama. There is a smile on Mama's face as Papa twirls her around. Fanny and Emily practically drag Henry and Philip onto the floor for the first dance. Rebecca looks truly content, dancing with Mr. Connelly.

From behind, a hand rests on Kate's shoulder. She can smell the whisky and cigars without even turning around. Her mood immediately turns foul.

"Shall we, Katherine?" Mr. O'Brien says, standing far too close. "The dance has just begun."

"Of course," she says. She catches Hugh's eye as she walks to the dance floor.

O'Brien skilfully leads her across the floor.

"You are such a beauty," he says, so close to her ear, his moustache feels like sharp pins sticking into her cheek.

"But I am much more than just beauty, Mr. O'Brien."

He laughs loudly. "Is that right?" Others look over. He's mocking her. She tries to resist as he pulls her even closer. "Your birthday is quickly approaching, is it not?"

"A few months off yet."

She's sure O'Brien will arrange a meeting with Papa well before her birthday, to ask for her hand in marriage. The whole population of Victoria knows this. Even Hugh. There is no turning back. Dread seeps into every cell of her body.

When the dance is over, O'Brien bows and Kate curtseys. "You must save the last dance for me, Katherine. I am sure it would please your mother immensely."

Kate turns her back and doesn't respond. Yes, it would

please Mama. But Mama's pleasure is not all that needs to be considered. For the rest of the evening, Kate mostly sits out the dancing; she has lost her verve and excitement for the night. And it hasn't helped, watching Hugh dance with almost every eligible young woman on the ship, including Rebecca, as well as the woman with the red feather in her hair. He has barely glanced her way. Does he believe there is more to her than just her beauty? Or maybe he is just playing with her. Kate wonders where her deep, festering envy comes from.

The last dance of the night. A waltz, of course. She tries to hide behind a group of tall men talking about the steady price of gold, but O'Brien moves toward her. She wishes she could refuse him, but that would surely cause a scandal. It certainly would with Mama. Maybe it is finally time to stand her ground. When O'Brien is a few strides away, Rebecca steps in front of him, takes his arm, and guides him to the dance floor. He looks hesitant at first, but reluctantly acquiesces. She turns and winks at Kate. Hugh appears right before her, like an apparition, holding his arm out for her.

"I sense a conspiracy," Kate says.

"Perhaps," says Hugh, as he leads her to the dance floor. "Are you complaining?"

"Not in the least."

It is clear Rebecca is trying to distract O'Brien with her wit and charm, but still he glares in Kate's direction as the waltz begins.

Her heart drums on her ribs. Where Kate's body touches Hugh's—her hand, her back, the brush of his leg against her dress—it is like smoldering fires shooting sparks to her every nerve. His eyes are the color of moss. Kate stares into them for the entire dance.

While the Captain wishes the guests goodnight, Hugh pulls out a small envelope from his uniform pocket and hands it to Kate.

"Until we meet again, my beautiful Kate." His hand lingers in hers before he goes to the stage to join his fellow officers, who are lined up, bowing and waving goodbye to the guests.

Kate hurries out on the deck, away from prying eyes, and opens the card. Inside is a plain simple heart with handwriting.

*The words to express my love are written on your heart.*

*Yours forever, Hugh*

# Chapter 15

Mama removes long strings of bejeweled necklaces, earrings, and pendants from the small drawers of a wooden jewelry chest. She places them on her bed.

"The rubies must go first, as they will sell for the highest price," she says, very business-like, as if she's sorting through produce at the market. "And some of the gold could be melted down for other purposes."

Kate holds out her emerald jewelry from O'Brien. "Take this, too, Mama."

"I won't sell those exquisite gems Mr. O'Brien gave you."

"But, Mama, I insist. This necklace and earrings could sell for a very high price."

Mama holds up the jewelry and looks at it admiringly for a long moment. Adds it to the others.

"But will this be enough?" Kate asks. "Will selling off this jewelry prevent the sale of our home?"

Mama shrugs. "It will hold off the creditors in the short term, at least."

"Oh, Mama. This must be so difficult for you," Kate says, sitting on Mama's bed. "Much of this was passed down from your grandmama. How sad it must be to part with it."

"That's why I insisted we sell the furniture first." Mama glances sadly at the gems on her bed. "However, other than Mr. Bedwell, who deals in gems, I cannot think of one person in Victoria who would truly appreciate the value of these pieces. It would be different if I were living in London and attending society functions, where there is an appreciation for fashion and adornment."

"But still, it is a loss."

"I have experienced much greater losses, Katherine. But I had hoped to pass the jewelry down to you when you marry."

"Sparkling gems do not excite me the way they do other women. And ..." Kate hesitates, to muster courage, "perhaps I will never marry."

"Such nonsense. You will surely marry." Mama removes a pink topaz pendant from the chest and hands it to Kate.

"Tell me you don't admire this gem."

Kate holds the jewel up to the window and sees how the light reflects through it. "It is very beautiful."

Mama takes the topaz from Kate and looks at it closely, before adding it to the collection on the bed. "Speaking of marriage, who is the naval officer who could not take his eyes off you the entire evening at the Valentine's Party?"

It's been weeks since the party on the ship, and she's has been expecting Mama's lecture. She's surprised Mama has waited this long.

"Lieutenant Hugh Ashton."

"Who are his family? Where are they from?"

"Mama, I know very little about him."

"You saved him the last waltz of the night. You must know something about him."

Kate goes to the window. The sky is blue and clear. The warm spring air is slowly coaxing the alder and oak buds to open.

"All I know is, he is from Cambridge. Schooled in Berkshire."

"Eton College?"

"I am not sure, Mama."

"If so, his family must have means. Eton is a very reputable school."

"I know nothing of his family and their means."

Mama sits on the bed and gestures for Kate to join her.

"The wife of a naval officer is a very difficult life, Katherine."

"But Mama, I barely know this man."

"Hear me out. Naval wives must cope with being separated from their husbands for extended periods of time. They must rear and school their children alone. They are forced into financial and management responsibilities most wives of their class can avoid. All the while living with the very real fear that their husbands might never return home alive."

Kate has already thought of all these things, but it pains her to hear them expressed out loud. The HMS *Forward* has been at sea for weeks, and Kate can well imagine the longing of naval wives to know their husbands are safe and close to home. But surely true love makes these challenges just a little bit easier to endure.

"As I told you, Mama, I hardly know Lieutenant Ashton."

Lucy knocks on the open door, carries in a pile of folded clean laundry, and places it in the armoire. She is in awe at the jewelry lined up on the bed.

"Come, have a look, Lucy," Kate says. Lucy is possibly the one person in Victoria who could appreciate the beauty, if not the value, of Mama's jewels.

Lucy's dark eyes dart around the bed. She wears small earrings, silver twisted in the shape of a knot, that Kate thinks are surprisingly tasteful, even more so if they were polished. Lucy picks up a ruby earring and holds it to the light.

"Beautiful," Lucy says. She puts down the earring and leaves the room.

"You should not be tempting that girl," Mama says. "If I find even a chain bracelet missing ..."

"Lucy has been with us for months now. Have you noticed even one item missing from our household?"

"One never can be sure of any hired help."

Kate sighs heavily and stands.

"Please pay heed to my concerns, Katherine. When you make certain choices, there are consequences. You must prepare yourself for the kind of life that awaits you."

Kate walks out the door and down the hall to her room.

On her desk is a letter addressed to her, but she doesn't recognize the handwriting. The postmark reads San Francisco. Inside the envelope is a folded letter with Rebecca's name on it. A red wax stamp imprinted with MT seals the pages. Not Jeremiah Fortune's initials, but it surely must be from him. Rebecca will be overjoyed, and Kate is truly happy for her. But she can't help but feel dejected that she has heard not one word from Hugh in weeks.

Kate picks up *Jane Eyre* from her desk, fans the pages.

Breathes them in. Jane Eyre would not be a person to moon and pine for a man—not even Mr. Rochester—the way Kate does for Hugh. She opens the desk drawer, reaches in the back, and pulls out the Valentine's card from Hugh.

*The words to express my love are written on your heart.*

*Yours forever, Hugh*

Those words create a longing in Kate that she has never before experienced. She hides the card back inside the drawer and takes out a few sheets of writing paper. Dips her pen in the inkwell.

*12 March 1862*

*Dear Arthur,*

*Forgive me for not writing to you sooner, but so much has taken place these past months, and I am afraid to tell you that not all of my news is good.*

*The Harding family's financial fortunes have not improved. Having to service debts in England as well as pay a mortgage here has proven to be Papa's final financial ruin. Mama reminds him almost daily with her contemptuous manner and foul moods. Although I am not privy to any details, it weighs so very heavily on him, and I know Papa is too proud to ask Uncle Charles for help. I am sorry to tell you such difficult news, but I feel you have a right to know. We are now forced to sell off furniture (remember the walnut buffet with the beveled mirror?) and Mama's valuable jewelry, in order to keep up with debt repayments. We may even lose our house. That is, unless I agree to marry Eamonn O'Brien, but it is the furthest wish from my mind.*

*On a brighter note, I have met a dear and true friend. Yes, here in Victoria. Rebecca is unlike anyone I've ever met before. Being from an upper-class New York family, she is well educated, worldly, and wise beyond her years. She is both bold and vibrant, which is like an elixir to brighten my boring, dreary life. And her romantic notions constantly amuse me. She was exiled to Vancouver Island to escape a scandal (the details too tangled and sensational to relay) and lives with the Bennets, her aunt and uncle. Rebecca introduced me to a novel,* Jane Eyre *by Charlotte Brontë. Have you heard of it? Arthur, I was so caught up in the story, I read the entire book in one sitting, and then I started right back at page one again. The main character is intriguing.* Jane Eyre *challenges almost every institution of our society—including women's subordinate role. No wonder these notions caused such a stir when the book was published. Just read these eloquent words that speak so deeply to my heart:*

Women are supposed to be very calm generally: but women feel just as men feel; they need exercise for their faculties, and a field for their efforts, as much as their brothers do; they suffer from too rigid a restraint, too absolute a stagnation, precisely as men would suffer; and it is narrow-minded in their more privileged fellow-creatures to say that they ought to confine themselves to making puddings and knitting stockings, to playing on the piano and embroidering bags. It is thoughtless to condemn them, or laugh at them, if they seek to do more or learn more than custom has pronounced necessary for their sex.

*I have been diligent about my medical studies. It is true that textbooks and Papa's notes are my only teachers, but I am determined to "exercise my faculties as my brother has done," even though society may not be ready for it. And, my dear Arthur, I wish with every cell of my being that you are able to pursue your heart's desire and live in Paris as an artist, as you so wish.*

*Your loving sister,*

*K*

*P.S. I, too, have a romantic interest, but there is so little to tell at this point.*

*—And I forgot to mention to you that with the help of our housemaid Lucy—I delivered a baby for a poor, gold-seeking Polish couple!*

If Kate were truly honest with herself, she would have to admit that she has been much less diligent with her medical research in the past month. Daydreams of traveling with Hugh on the seven seas have crowded her thoughts. She once read about a naval wife, Elizabeth Wynne, who accompanied her husband on a warship during the Napoleonic Wars, and was even credited with nursing England's military war hero, Rear-Admiral Horatio Nelson, who lost his right arm in the British Assault on the Spanish Canary Islands.

Rebecca sits with Kate in the Hardings' sitting room, holding the letter. A waterfall of golden curls rests on her shoulders. Her hands are shaky.

"But I do not understand how his letter could have arrived so quickly. I sent him your address only a few short months ago."

"Are you not going to open it?" Kate asks.

"Of course. I am just mystified how this magic happened."

Rebecca opens the wax seal. Inside the outer page is a smaller piece of paper. "Western Union Telegraph Company." She looks up at Kate, then reads the note. Her eyes well up.

"Is everything all right?"

Rebecca nods; a tear spills down her cheek.

"Can you at least explain the magic of his timing?"

"Jeremiah sent two telegrams to San Francisco. One was written for me, and another to his friend, with instructions to mail this note to Victoria."

"I did not know the telegraph wires spanned from east to west," says Kate.

Rebecca reads the short note again. "He says he misses me dreadfully and is scheming a way for us to be together. By now he is in St. Lucia to initiate divorce proceedings with his wife."

Rebecca breaks down crying.

"But surely that is very good news," Kate says.

"The very best of news. I am weeping with relief and joy, dear Kate. I am sure Papa had Jeremiah ostracized from New York's business circles, and yet he still wishes to be with me. Never did I imagine in all my life I would experience such love and devotion."

A searing ache threatens to crack Kate wide open. First of all, if only Hugh would express such adoration to her, other than a few words written on a Valentine's card. But also, Kate cannot imagine the life that Rebecca and Jeremiah will have together. They will most certainly have to live on some tropical island, away from all of civilization, where their union would not be considered immoral as well as illegal. And if they had children, Kate is not sure how they would fare in such a cruel and unforgiving world.

# Chapter 16

"I'm surprised you haven't heard of Vogel's shop," Sister Mary says. She and Kate walk down the dusty road, past the livery stables reeking of manure and full of neighing horses. It's early morning and workmen unload large wagons of goods being delivered to grocers and import stores. "There are many treasures to be found, I assure you."

"Treasures or not, Mama does not like me to come to this area of Fort Street. Although I'm sure she would be at ease since I'm with you, Sister." In fact, Mama would be horrified to know that Sister Mary was taking Kate anywhere near, let alone patronizing, a business in this part of town. Kate can hear Mama clearly: *No so-called woman of God would ever be seen there. Surely, she does not respect herself or her religion.*

When they turn down Fort Street, Kate sees Lucy's aunty on the front porch of the brothel, among Chinese and other

Indian women dressed provocatively, trying to entice the scruffy miners and laborers gathered on the sidewalk.

"Poor lost souls," Sister Mary says as they pass. "May the Lord shower His grace and blessing upon them."

"The prostitutes or the miners?" The words blurt out of Kate's mouth without scrutiny.

Sister Mary gives her a weak smile. "Both."

A bell rings on the shop door when Kate and Sister Mary enter Vogel's Pawn Shop. Mr. Vogel sits behind a small desk, sorting through papers. His head, bald but for two stripes of frizzy brown hair, appears to have grown out of his chest rather than on top of his shoulders. When he looks up to see Sister Mary, he smiles, takes off his circular wire-framed glasses.

"*Guten Morgen*," he says.

"*Guten Morgen, Herr Vogel.*"

"*Wie geht es dir heute morgen*?" he asks.

Although Kate knows very little German, she does know he asked Sister Mary how she was this morning. They continue to exchange pleasantries in German, while Kate looks around the shop. Mama would never approve of her shopping in a used-goods store on the wrong side of Fort Street, where the lower classes spend their hard-earned money. But a nun seems to have no problem buying goods here, at a much-reduced price, for the school, for the Sisters of St. Ann's residence, or for her.

The air smells thick and musty. Scattered around the floor and on tables in no apparent order are old, well-used items such as household kitchen goods, hand tools, small furniture, guitars and violins with missing strings, and children's toys, such as dolls, spinning tops, and toy soldiers. A cabinet is filled with inexpensive commonplace gems. Lucy must have been a regular customer here. In one corner of the shop, two men wearing suspenders that hold up their baggy trousers sort through the scant supply of pickaxes, shovels, drills, and pans. Kate wonders if there will be any Cariboo gold left for them to mine.

"Is there anything I can help you with today?" Mr. Vogel asks.

"I wanted to show Katherine the shipment of books that recently arrived," Sister Mary says. "I would like to purchase a few textbooks for her."

"By all means." Mr. Vogel puts on his glasses and attends to his papers.

Sister Mary leads Kate down a narrow dark hallway to the back of the store. In a small dusty room, lit with only a small sliver of a window, are shelves of books, piled from floor to ceiling. Sister Mary scours one shelf and pulls out a thick book with a ragged black leather cover, and hands it to Kate—*The Diseases of Women with Child and in Child Bearing* by Francis Maruiceau. Kate opens the cover and sees that it was published in 1710.

"How did such a book end up in Victoria?" she asks.

"Mr. Vogel receives shipments of books from all over the world." Sister Mary continues, looking through the titles. "There are a few more medical textbooks, but most are written in German. However, I did find one other that may interest you." She keeps searching through the stacks. "Ah, here it is. *A Syllabus of Lectures on Midwifery* by Dr. John Haighton, published 1811." She hands it to Kate.

Sister Mary's encouragement has planted a seed of hope, and the root is beginning to germinate. When she's with Sister Mary, Kate feels like her future ambitions are somehow possible, that is, until she finds herself alone and stewing with her dark thoughts.

"Look here. A box of novels just arrived," Sister Mary says, pointing to a box on the floor. "Choose whichever ones you like."

"So generous of you, Sister."

Kate bends down and reads the titles, including, *The Count of Monte Cristo*, *Ivanhoe*, *Oliver Twist*, *Persuasion*, *The Pickwick Papers*. She has read many of them, but then spots a book she hasn't read—*Wuthering Heights* by Emily Brontë. Surely this writer must be related to Charlotte Brontë, author of *Jane Eyre*. She takes the novel out of the box and adds it to her two obstetrics textbooks.

Sister Mary pays for the books that Mr. Vogel has wrapped in brown paper. Kate glances at a table by the front window. Hidden among old clocks with rusty faces is a large jewelry box painted turquoise, with an ivory cameo inset on the lid. Kate blows off the dust and opens it. The inside is lined with red velvet and divided by removable compartments. And although there is no twirling figurine, when a tiny key is turned, a tinkling Mozart concerto plays. She digs in her purse and counts the coins. Just enough.

Kate sits at her bedroom desk, poring over the textbooks Sister Mary bought for her, and recording the new knowledge in a notebook, especially intended for her study of obstetrics. Drawings and diagrams of the stages of the fetus fascinate her. She reads about signs of pregnancy, labor, birth, and post-delivery. One curious passage states that working-class women are delivered on top of the bed sheets, while upper-class are delivered beneath. But why? Are working-class women to be treated with less propriety than upper-class women?

A full chapter of one textbook is devoted to female hysteria, since female nervous disorders are directly connected to a woman's reproductive organs. The primary cause of hysteria, the text says, is the overuse of the female mind. She must ask Papa his opinion about whether a female who uses her mental faculties is at risk of hysteria. Kate knows that exercising her intellect is all that is keeping her sanity intact. Treatment of hysteria includes months-long bed rest, with no mentally strenuous activities, such as reading and writing. The text writes that women with this condition must save all their energy, in order to fulfill their duties as wives and mothers. The text suggests ovariotomies (removal of the ovaries) and hysterectomies (removal of the uterus) may be needed in some cases of hysteria, and for extreme symptoms, women are to be admitted into insane asylums. Kate believes that perhaps the reason women become hysterical is because of their lack of choices in life. When women are counseled to suppress their intellectual capabilities, this may be the true cause of mental instability. But who is she to question the scholarship of learned men?

Outside, James's cheery laughter can be heard. She looks out the window to see him riding on poor Lucy's back like a jockey, as she gallops her way up the drive. He finally slips off her back and they hold hands, spin each other around until both fall on the ground laughing. Kate closes her eyes and imagines Hugh holding her hands, spinning her, the world swirling around so all that remains is the two of them. A feeling of pure joy washes over her. Then she opens her eyes and reality stings like a slap.

Footsteps rumble up the stairs. She hears Lucy tell James to play in his room. A knock on her door.

"Come in."

Lucy has a look on her face that she can't read.

"What is it, Lucy?"

Lucy sticks her hand in her skirt pocket, pulls out a small piece of paper, and hands it to Kate.

Kate unfolds the paper and reads.

> *Meet me on the same beach near Ogden Point where I met you before. I will be waiting for you there. All day and night if I must.*
>
> *Lovingly, Hugh*

"When did he give this to you?"

"He was waiting on the bridge as I walked into town."

An unexpected fury builds inside Kate like a lit cannon full of gunpowder. "Did you not think this was important enough to bring it to me sooner?" Her voice is loud and sharp. "I saw you dilly-dallying up the drive, playing with James. I cannot imagine why you wouldn't have run right back home as quickly as your legs would take you! What is wrong with you?"

Lucy's bottom lip quivers and her eyes fill with tears. With hands on her hips, Kate takes several deep breaths.

"Oh, Lucy, I am truly sorry." Kate takes Lucy's hands. "I did not mean to speak so crossly. I have waited for word from Lieutenant Ashton for weeks, and I am frustrated, not because of you, but by my own silly notions. Please forgive me."

Lucy looks at her suspiciously, but nods.

Kate looks at herself in the mirror. Strands of frizzy hair stick wildly out of her head.

"I look a fright."

"Sit," Lucy says. She wipes a tear from her cheek with her apron. She picks up a comb and hairpins, while Kate sits in front of her vanity. While Lucy works on her hair, Kate pinches her cheeks to pink them up.

"Thank you, Lucy. Again, please accept my apology. But I must ask that you not say a word about this note to Mama." Kate is certain Lucy will keep this secret. Given Mama's brusque manner, which she herself has obviously inherited, Lucy rarely speaks to Mama unless spoken to.

Lucy turns to leave.

"Wait, I have something for you." Kate picks up the jewelry box beside her desk and hands it to Lucy.

Lucy's eyes widen as she examines the outside of the box. She looks closely at the cameo on the lid.

"Open it up," Kate says. "I'm afraid it does not have the spinning ballerina, but it does play music. See?" Kate turns the key.

Lucy opens the box and the music plays. She runs her fingers over the red velvet.

"I'm sure with all the jewelry you have collected, you will make a very good match," Kate says. Lucy explores the box, takes out the two top compartments to see a hidden level beneath, also covered in red velvet.

"I'd better go quickly," Kate says, looking in the mirror once more. "He may have given up on me by now."

"He will be there," Lucy says.

Lucy follows as Kate hurries down the stairs, holding

Hugh's note. As she pulls her coat off the hook, Mama appears in the foyer. Kate quickly stuffs the note into her coat pocket.

"Where are you off to, Katherine?"

"Just for a walk, Mama. I've been reading in my room all morning and into the afternoon. I am desperate for some fresh air." Her voice is shaky. She talks too fast. Mama looks at her questioningly.

"If it is fresh air you need, you can walk with me to the Merricks'. I will get the basket."

No! Not now.

Kate sighs, slowly puts on her coat. "Of course, Mama."

"Please, Mrs. Harding," Lucy says. "I go instead. Last time I became attached to her children."

"Then the three of us will visit Mrs. Merrick," Mama says emphatically.

Lucy and Kate share a look.

"There is not space for three guests," Lucy says, shaking her head.

Mama observes Kate for a long moment. She must know Kate is hiding something. "I am sure Mrs. Merrick will be most happy to welcome us all."

After crossing the bridge, they turn down Humboldt Street, also known as Kanaka Row. The inlet on the town side of James Bay reeks of horse dung and privies that haven't been emptied often enough. It turns Kate's stomach, and she covers her face with the collar of her coat. Mama walks down the street confidently, her head held high, as they pass mostly men wearing shabby garb and menacing stares. Most likely miners who never struck gold. The Merrick home must have been an old Kanaka dwelling; it looks more like a shed and is even smaller than Nora's barn. Newborn cries and toddler squeals can be heard from inside. Kate looks at the sun that is getting lower in the western sky. She doubts Hugh will wait for her all night, as he wrote in his note.

Mama knocks on the door. There is a big gap at the bottom, as if a large wild animal had taken a bite out of the wood. Mrs. Merrick opens the door, holding her baby boy, who is wiggling and crying fretfully. Clumps of hair hang down around her ashen face, and her dress is streaked with dirt and faded with wear.

"We have brought you a basket, Mrs. Merrick," Mama says.

Tears immediately pour down Mrs. Merrick's face. "You are angels sent directly from the good Lord himself," she says, her body shaking in relief. "The pantry is near empty."

She steps aside and they enter. The one room has a stove in the corner; the wall behind it is blackened with soot. Beds are against the opposite wall. Two small, scruffy boys sit on the dirty floor, playing with the kindling. The oldest daughter is curled up in one of the beds. Lucy places the basket on the rickety table, takes the crying baby from Mrs. Merrick, and rocks him in her arms. While Mama and Mrs. Merrick sit at the small table, Kate sits on the bed with the girl. Her face is red, and when Kate feels her forehead, it is hot and sweaty.

"Mrs. Merrick," Kate says, "how long has your daughter been ill?"

"Eilonwyn's been not right going on three days now."

Kate feels the child's neck and finds her glands are swollen. A rash covers her body.

"Open your mouth for me," Kate says, "that's a good girl." The child's tongue is red and lumpy.

"Mrs. Merrick, I am concerned Eilonwyn has scarlet fever."

"Do not alarm Mrs. Merrick, Katherine," Mama says. "The girl has not yet been examined by a doctor."

"I am sure of the symptoms, Mama. We must send Papa here immediately."

Kate watches at the surgery door as Papa puts his doctor's bag in the carriage and climbs in.

"Walk on," he says to Nora, and waves to Kate as the carriage bumps down the road.

Lucy enters the surgery and hands Kate her coat and bonnet.

"Go now," Lucy says.

"I am most sure he will not still be waiting, Lucy."

"I am most sure he will."

Kate ponders for a long moment.

The sun has all but set over the Sooke hills. Kate passes near Ogden Point, sees smoke rise from the wooden huts in the temporary Haida Village. She climbs down the bluff to the beach, where the air is saturated with the stench of a rotting dead seal. She breathes through her mouth as she clambers over rocks and driftwood, as the waves lap the pebbly shoreline. From a distance, she sees someone stand. Soon, she recognizes Hugh's big smile. He jogs toward her, wearing the same brown day suit he wore last time they met on this beach. She places a hand on her chest to quiet her pounding heart.

When he's close, he takes her hands in his and studies her face. "You are a picture of heaven." He kisses both her hands. "I wasn't sure if my note would find you, and if it did, I wasn't sure you would come."

"Why would I not come?"

"Being out at sea for weeks, I have not been the most attentive suitor."

Suitor? Did he really use that word? Does he mean it?

"No need to worry, Lieutenant Ashton. I have not exactly been standing at the window, waiting for your ship to sail into Victoria Harbour."

Looking deflated, he lets go of her hands. "Of course, I didn't presume you were."

Why must she sound so harsh and crusty? And, in fact, she's a liar. She *has* been waiting for his ship, every hour of every single day.

"I only meant that I manage to keep myself occupied. Even in this sleepy town."

"Yes, of course." Now Hugh seems very nervous. He gestures to a log where they both sit.

"How long will the HMS *Forward* remain in Victoria?" Kate asks.

"A month? A week? A day? A lowly lieutenant never knows until just a few days before orders are given." Hugh looks down at his folded hands in his lap. "Kate, I have not stopped thinking of you—your vivacity, your intelligence—and, of course, your beautiful image has not left my mind's eye since the day I met you on that ridiculous plank walkway. In fact, you distract my thoughts away from my tasks aboard ship—so much so that I fear I may even make a fatal mistake."

So, he feels the same? He's been longing for her as much as she has for him?

"Will the navy be your career?" She sounds so matter of fact, but it's a question she has wanted to ask.

Hugh looks out into the strait. "After graduating Eton, I had my sights on studying law at Cambridge or Oxford. I joined the Royal Navy mainly to please my father. He wanted at least one of his sons to fulfill the ambition that he had never managed to. As the eldest son, he chose me. I was most certain I would hate it. But after four years of officer training at the Royal Navy College at Dartmouth, and four years at sea, I have come to love this life. And frankly, I can't imagine another career that would be as satisfying. I suppose I have my father to thank. And I have been told that with hard work, I will very soon climb the ranks and earn the commission of Captain."

"It must be rewarding to be able to chart your own life and see success in your future."

He turns to her, looks deep into her eyes. “Yes, it is rewarding. But my life will amount to nothing if you are not a part of it. I know that to the very depths of my being.”

“But what of my own ambitions?” The words come out too quickly.

Hugh is taken aback. “I don’t know what you mean.” Of course, he doesn’t. What man would?

“Perhaps I need more in my life than to be just a wife and mother.”

“Then I will support you as best I can.” She doesn’t fully believe him. His words sound halting, and he doesn’t even ask for clarification. “Dear Kate. I am a young man who can’t offer near the fortune that someone like Mr. O’Brien can. And it will be, at the very least, two years before I can marry and provide you a proper home. But if you will have me, Kate, I assure you, I will be the most loving and devoted husband.”

Kate’s very soul rips apart in different directions. Looking into Hugh’s eyes, she feels love like she has never before experienced. This may be her only chance at true happiness with a man. But she has a life, too. Perhaps she has deluded herself into thinking that she could actually study medicine at a university. And what about her family? Would she stand by and watch as they fell even further into financial ruin, or should she accept O'Brien's proposal so her whole family would benefit? She can't very well ask Hugh how much he's worth.

Kate holds her head in both hands, trying to calm the swirling thoughts.

"Do you at least share my love?" Hugh asks.

"Yes, I share your love." These words are difficult to speak. She constantly feels she must protect herself.

"Then you will wait for me?"

Kate tries to pull out the best answer from her jumbled thoughts.

"That I cannot promise."

By the disheartened look on Hugh's face, it obviously was not what he had hoped she would say.

"I am sorry I cannot give you a definite answer, Hugh. There is much to consider. I need time to sort out what will be best for me, and possibly for my family."

"Know that I will wait for your decision. For the rest of my life, if I must." Hugh wraps his arms around her and kisses her deeply. Kate feels like her world has dropped away and she is being carried on a cloud.

# Chapter 17

As Kate lies in bed in the dark, she replays the meeting with Hugh over and over in her mind. She tries to remember his every word and gesture. She touches her lips, remembering the feel of his kisses. So gentle, yet passionate. How could this be anything but pure love? She closes her eyes and wills herself to dream of him, as she slowly falls asleep.

*She walks down the forest path carpeted with moss, surrounded by ancient trees. The loon's screeching call is faint at first but becomes louder, the nearer she moves toward the ocean. She knows she is there to meet Hugh. She looks all around but doesn't see him. The loon's haunting cry suddenly stops. Hugh walks out from the water like a ghostly Poseidon, holding the loon in his hands. Its body is limp, neck broken, drooping over his arm. Hugh is dispassionate as he shows Kate the dead bird. But the loon's red eye once again emits a piercing sting into her chest that takes Kate's breath away.*

She wakes. Another terrifying dream about the loon. But also about Hugh. She fumbles in the dark to light a candle and paces her room. In her dream, Hugh carried the dead loon. By marrying him, she would most definitely have to give up her desire to pursue medical studies. This is the decision that would haunt her for the rest of her life. Is this what the loon is trying to tell her?

After a morning of reading *Wuthering Heights* in her bedroom, Kate concludes the story is as romantic and tragic as *Romeo and Juliet*, and as revengeful as *Hamlet*. She can't help but make some comparisons to the tangled love with the three suitors in her own life—Mr. O'Brien, Hugh, and medicine.

She descends the stairs and hears voices behind closed doors in the dining room. She tiptoes down the last creaky steps and presses her ear against the door.

"I'm afraid there are no other options, Louisa. The bank has made it clear they will not extend our credit again."

Lucy, with an armful of clean, folded sheets, walks down the hallway and stops when she hears the voices in the other room. Kate puts her finger to her lips for Lucy to remain quiet. Lucy continues up the stairs.

"But this house is all we have, William. Where we live with our children. I have worked hard to make it a warm and inviting home in this godforsaken place."

"I am desperately sorry I have failed you and the family. But we must move forward as best we can."

"What are we to do now? Where will we live?"

"I have spoken to Mr. Reed. He has expressed interest in purchasing the house, and he has a few houses to rent out. I have to warn you right now, Louisa, they are much smaller and more modest than this one."

So, it has come to this. They will soon move out of the only house Kate has known since moving to Victoria.

"Such humiliation." Mama cries, blowing her nose loudly. "Can we not just go back to London, where we have always belonged?"

"Moving back to England is not possible. It would take me years to build a medical practice there."

Surely Mama must have known that would never be an option. Kate hears her sobbing.

"There, there, my dear." Kate imagines Papa awkwardly patting Mama's back. He has always struggled to show his affection to her. Could be because she is often as prickly as a sea urchin.

"Has Mr. O'Brien asked your permission to propose to Katherine?"

"Yes, he has, and I granted him that permission."

Kate feels like a shard of ice has pierced deep into her chest.

"But, my dear ... " Papa says, "we cannot count on Kitty to pull us out of our debts. She should be the one to choose whom she wishes to marry."

"She has some silly notion that she may never marry."

"Then that should be her choice. And hers alone."

But Kate now knows what her choice must be.

The sweet scent of cherry pipe tobacco meanders down the hallway, as Kate makes her way to the surgery. She hears Papa and another man speaking. Sounds like Governor Douglas. He must have come in through the surgery door. She quietly inches closer to hear their conversation.

"With no coordinated public health agency, I'm asking you and John to take up the cause for the colony. I know from experience how devastating this disease can be. Especially to the Indians. Measures must be taken immediately to prevent the spread of the infection."

What is this disease that Papa and Dr. Helmcken are tasked with preventing? A chair scrapes and footsteps creak across the wooden floor.

"There is no time to waste, I'm afraid. I will sign off on any provisions you need." The surgery door opens to the outside. Kate can feel the cool breeze.

"I will do my best, Governor." The door closes, clicks to lock.

Kate waits a few minutes before entering the surgery. Papa puffs on his pipe as he writes into a ledger. The candle has almost burned down, casting an eerie glow on his face.

"You need more light, Papa?" she says, and places the candle she carried in on the desk. "And what is it that keeps you working so late?"

"It appears that the steamship *Brother Jonathan* from San Francisco unloaded more than just sixty tons of freight and one hundred passengers. It also left behind the varioloid virus.

"Smallpox?"

"Yes, two passengers have fallen ill with the disease. I am ordering more vaccine that I hope will prevent an outbreak. With all the shipping activity between San Francisco and Victoria, it was only a matter of time before the disease reached our shores."

"Should we be worried?"

"Yes, and we must do everything we can to contain it. I implored Governor Douglas to quarantine the Indians in the Northerners' Encampment, but my request fell on deaf ears."

"What would a quarantine do, Papa?"

"Quarantine prevents exposure to people who may be contagious."

Papa goes to his cabinet and searches through his bottles. "Sit and pull up your left sleeve." Kate does so and he takes out a small bottle. "We are short on serum." Papa wipes alcohol on her upper arm. He then picks up a sharp knife-like tool and scrapes a layer of her skin and applies the vaccine. It stings. "Immunity decreases after five years, so at least I can make sure my family is revaccinated before it runs out. I will vaccinate James and your mama this evening, as well." He daubs the drops of blood with gauze and tapes it in place. She rolls down her sleeve, stands, and begins pacing the room.

"What is it, Kitty? Is something on your mind?"

"I have made a decision, Papa. If marrying Mr. O'Brien will save our home and pay off our debts, I will do it." She tries to quell the sick churning in her stomach.

"We will manage through this, Kitty. I will not have you sacrifice your own happiness."

She kneels at his feet. "But you make sacrifices each day, Papa. You work so very hard in this community, such long hours, and provide care to so many people. And I know sometimes you don't even charge for your services." Papa looks at her—he's been found out. "If marrying O'Brien will make life better for you, Mama, Arthur, and James, then it's a sacrifice I will happily make. Is that not what the Christian doctrine states? To lay down one's life for others?"

Papa smiles weakly and cups his hand on her cheek.

"Such strength and wisdom for a woman so young. As you know, Kitty, such a choice is irreversible."

"I do know that, Papa, and I will not be deterred."

"I just ask that you do not make this decision in haste."

"I have pondered it the entire day. I know my own mind."

"That you do." He reaches down and holds Kate tightly in his arms.

If she is haunted the rest of her life, so be it.

Bright sun pours through the surgery window. James sits on the examining table with his sleeve rolled up. Kate looks on while Papa prepares to give her brother the vaccine.

"Will it hurt, Papa?" James asks.

"It will hurt, but only for a time," Papa says, taking a bottle of serum off his shelf.

"Papa, please show me how, and I will vaccinate James," Kate says.

"Your mama is due in here at any moment for her own vaccination. If she sees you with the lancet in your hand, she will be very unhappy with me."

"Please, just let me hold it and you guide my hand." Kate gives him her best pleading expression.

Papa always loses these battles with her. He hands Kate the knife-like instrument. "You must scrape the outer layers of the epidermis." He guides her hand that grazes James's skin.

"Ouch! That hurts," James says.

"Almost done," Kate says. "You are a brave boy."

Papa then applies the serum to an ivory point and hands it to her.

"Make sure you cover the scraped area with the serum," Papa says.

Kate uses the point to apply the vaccine. Joy bubbles up from deep inside her.

Kate and Rebecca walk arm-in-arm down the road past the Bennet home that separates town from country. After an overnight rain, the pungent smell of damp earth and manure blows on a warm breeze. Mooing cows and frolicking horses dot the distant fields.

"I do not think my heart and soul are even half as noble and selfless as yours," Rebecca says.

"My decision to marry Eamonn O'Brien is only part of my sorrow. It appears fate has played a very cruel joke on me." Kate reaches in her coat pocket, pulls out a letter and hands it to Rebecca. "I received this letter only one day after accepting O'Brien's proposal."

Rebecca reads.

*New York, USA*

*February 22, 1862*

*Miss Katherine Harding*

*2 Kingston Street*

*Victoria, Colony of Vancouver Island*

*Dear Miss Harding,*

*There is only one Infirmary for Poor Women and Children in New York City, so your letter indeed found me.*

*I am truly sorry about the despair you have been experiencing. In some ways, you remind me of myself as a young woman. I was also desperate for some object in life that would stimulate my intellect, fill the emptiness in my soul, and prevent the sad wearing away of my heart.*

*You may be interested to know that, unlike you, medicine was the last profession I ever thought I would pursue. I was initially repulsed by everything connected with the human body and could not bear the sight of a medical book. I was much more interested in studying history and metaphysics, and therefore began my career as a teacher, which is, of course, considered more suitable for a woman. It wasn't until my close friend was dying, and because she was too embarrassed to go to a male doctor, suggested she would have suffered less if her physician had been a woman. That affected me deeply and changed the course of my life.*

*I was told by several physicians known to my family that it was impossible for me to attend medical school—it was too expensive and this education was not available to women. I convinced two physician friends to tutor me in medical studies, while I applied to all medical schools in New York, Philadelphia, and many more in the northeast states. I was finally accepted at Geneva Medical College in western New York State in 1847. And you are mistaken about one thing you wrote. I am not the only woman physician in the United States. My sister, Dr. Emily Blackwell, also earned her medical degree in 1854 from Western Reserve University in Cleveland, Ohio. Together we opened the New York Infirmary.*

*It has not been easy being a pioneer but, oh, it has been fascinating! I would not trade one moment, even the worst moment I have endured, for all the riches in the world. It has been a great moral struggle, but this moral fight was an immense attraction for me. It has been my assertion that if society will not admit women's free intellectual, economic, and professional development, then society must be refashioned.*

*My advice for you? Pursue your passion with all of your strength. But I must warn you, Miss Harding. Being both a woman and physician is not for the faint of heart. There is much social and professional antagonism facing women physicians that can leave one without support, respect, or professional counsel. It can be a lonely life, indeed.*

*If you find yourself in New York City, I would be most happy to meet with you and have you tour the clinic. Until that day arrives, hold tightly to your dreams.*

*Yours faithfully,*

*Dr. Elizabeth Blackwell*

"Oh, my dear, sweet Kate. No wonder you are in such anguish." She wraps an arm firmly around Kate's shoulder.

“What am I to do, Rebecca? How can I pursue my passion with all my strength, as Elizabeth Blackwell encourages me to do, and then leave my family destitute? And what about Hugh? He is the man I truly love.”

“Does he know of your decision?”

“Not yet. The thought is too painful. It will make it seem all too real, somehow.”

“You are truly in the most difficult of quandaries. I wish there were some way to help you through this.”

Kate rests her head on Rebecca’s shoulder as they continue down the road.

“Being the true and dear friend that you are helps more than you will ever know.”

# Chapter 18

Cheealthluc, wearing his signature navy uniform jacket, crowds his queen, princesses, and his usual entourage into Papa's surgery. The door remains open, and a line of other Songish people snake outside the surgery, around the side of the house. Kate doesn't see Old Pierre in the line, and, much to Mama's annoyance, Lucy is off harvesting camas with the women in her family. She won't be back for several days.

"Our medicine people say no. Not good for our people," Cheealthluc says with a resolute tone. "We have our own remedies."

"With all due respect," Papa says, "the only way to prevent this deadly disease is by inoculation or vaccination. And by quarantine–isolating your people from the disease. If not, your entire people could be at risk of extermination."

"The whole reserve could die?"

"Yes, everyone–men, women, and children. Smallpox

does not discriminate. It spreads from one person to another and even on contaminated objects such as clothing, bedding, or blankets."

Cheealthluc's face falls. He turns and translates to those around him.

"There is a two-week incubation period after contracting the disease," Papa explains. "This means the symptoms do not show for two weeks."

Cheealthluc nods.

"The first symptoms include a high fever, headache, body pain, and perhaps nausea and vomiting." Papa gestures in order to make himself understood. "Two weeks after the first exposure to the virus, a rash begins on the face, hands, and feet. Then it spreads to the whole body. The rash then turns to red spots or bumps, which in turn become lesions or blisters. In the worst cases, the lesions cover the entire body and blindness may occur in one or both eyes."

"How long to end?" Cheealthluc asks.

"It takes about one month for the disease to run its course."

"After vaccine, then no more disease?"

"Even after having received the vaccine, one in fifty people may still contract the disease. But if no one is vaccinated, the smallpox will spread and most of your people will die."

Cheealthluc's usual jovial expression has turned grave. He confers with those around him and they talk for several minutes. Finally ...

"We will take the medicine."

"You have made a wise choice. But only some of your people are here today. I will have to come to the reserve as well, along with Dr. Helmcken."

"I will arrange."

Kate had begged Papa to let her be a part of this meeting with the Songish. Now she must beg him to let her help him vaccinate these people. She pulls bottles of vaccine out of a box.

"Papa, if you let me help, we can vaccinate this group in half the time. You have already shown me how with James."

"Kitty, this is my work alone."

Kate looks at him imploringly. "I want to help. I *need* to help."

He sighs deeply. "If you are so determined, I am powerless to refuse you, Kitty."

"Then let us begin, shall we?" She asks those in the surgery to bare one of their upper arms for the vaccine.

The exhilaration from working with Papa dissolves with each step up to her room. Resigned and resolute, she knows what she must do. She sits at her desk with paper and ink.

*Dear Hugh,*

*It is with a heavy heart that I write to you, but you must hear this news directly from me. I have accepted Mr. O'Brien's proposal of marriage. This decision was made not out of love (very far from it) but out of expediency. I can no longer sit by and watch my family fall further into bankruptcy. Mr. O'Brien's promise of immediate rescue is our only hope.*

*Although it will most likely be of little consolation, know that you are the only man I love.*

*If only fate had brought us together under different circumstances. I wish you only the very best. May you always be safe on your sea journeys.*

*With love,*

*Kate*

She puts down her pen and looks out the window. The

HMS *Forward*, which she has come to recognize, is at anchor in the harbor. She wonders if Hugh really is her true love. If she were given the choice between marriage to Hugh and acceptance into medical school, which one would she choose? Where would her heart lead her?

But those are just fanciful musings. Her fate is now sealed. She puts the note in an envelope and will send Lucy to deliver it.

Kate feels like an observer, detached from her body and floating near the ceiling, as she looks around at the room decorated with white ribbons and bows, and full of guests gathered to celebrate her engagement to Mr. O'Brien. He has brought his legion of fair-skinned Irish housemaids, in crisp white uniforms with black aprons, to help serve the food and drinks to the guests, while Lucy is meant to be out of sight, banished to the kitchen to clean up the mess.

Rebecca takes her hand, which brings her attention back down to Earth, and closely inspects the ring. "I have never before seen a gem quite so enormous," she says. Kate thinks the Ceylon sapphire, encircled with diamonds and as large as a shilling coin, looks almost comical on her thin finger.

"He spared no expense—you must give him that."

"I'm sure the cost of this ring alone would pay off our house debt," Kate says.

Rebecca, in a stunning pale peach dress with a matching ribbon around the waist, her blonde hair perfectly twisted and braided, looks more like the bride-to-be than she does. Rather than order an expensive tailor-made dress from San Francisco, Kate insisted on choosing one from her wardrobe—a gown the color of a bluebird that Mama thought much too loud and unfashionable for such a special occasion. Still, ever since Kate accepted O'Brien's proposal, Mama's mood has been manic, her face etched in a permanent smile. She flits between O'Brien, the Bennets, the Flemings, the Pembertons, the Trutches, and Justice Begbie. Papa is more subdued; he's not convinced Kate made the right decision. Neither is she, but what's done is done.

She walks around the room to accept congratulations from the guests. The women swoon over her ring and the men bow in respect. On her rounds, she overhears a conversation between Mr. Trutch and Mr. Pemberton.

"The filth and squalor on the reserve and in the encampments will only cause the disease to spread faster," Trutch says.

"Between Drs. Harding and Helmcken, and Reverend

Garret and Bishop Hills, great strides are being made to vaccinate the various tribes," Pemberton replies.

Trutch takes an angry gulp of whiskey from his glass. "If smallpox only spread among the Indians, it would rid our community of its moral ulcer, but our own population is greatly at risk. Is it not time to remove every native from our vicinity?"

"With Douglas away," Pemberton says, "it seems the colonial government is paralyzed. As Superintendent of Police, it rests on my shoulders to search out and remove those whose condition is detrimental to the health of the population."

"And I assume force will be used against them, if required. Surely the colonial interests must be preserved at all costs."

"I have contacted the captains of both HMS *Grappler* and the HMS *Forward*. They have agreed to assist in any way necessary."

Any way necessary? Surely Hugh would not agree to forcibly remove natives from Victoria. The warships could use their armaments to bombard the villages and encampments. Kate suddenly feels lightheaded.

The Reverend Fleming tinkles his glass with a spoon and

everyone quiets down. O'Brien sidles up to Kate. Red and purple blood vessels slither like tiny snakes across his face and nose. The coal tar and rosewater cologne doesn't mask the strong odor of whiskey on his breath.

His lips touch her ear. "You will have no regrets, this I assure you, Katherine. I will mostly leave you alone unless I need you on my arm or in my bed." Her whole body shudders. He takes her left hand, thumbs the large jewel.

"Flora and I would like to express our most enthusiastic congratulations to Miss Katherine Harding and Mr. Eamonn O'Brien for their wedding engagement," the Reverend says. "I would like to propose a toast."

As everyone raises glasses, Kate catches Rebecca's sympathetic look.

"May you find much happiness together, provide one another with the love and comfort you both so richly deserve, and bring many healthy children into the world."

"To Katherine and Eamonn!" Everyone chimes in with glasses raised.

Mama looks more radiant than Kate has seen her in years. She wears a beautiful silk gown—black, of course. Her blue eyes sparkle. Will Mama's happiness make this sacrifice worth it?

At the end of the evening, when most of the guests have left, Kate goes to the kitchen to check on Lucy. Housemaids scurry in with trays of dirty dishes and glasses, while O'Brien, chest puffed out like a peacock, stands too close to Lucy. She looks fearful; her gaze rests on the floor.

"Why on earth are you in the kitchen, Mr. O'Brien?" Kate asks.

He turns around nonchalantly. "I was just checking on the staff I hired for this merry occasion. At great expense, mind you."

Lucy's gaze doesn't leave the floor.

"Is it not time to call me by my Christian name, Katherine?" His glance lingers on Lucy before he swaggers out of the kitchen.

"Is everything all right, Lucy?" Kate asks.

Lucy brushes past her, lifts a heavy bucket of water onto the stove to boil.

Kate has witnessed O'Brien staring at Lucy in the past. She can only imagine what he said that upset her so.

# Chapter 19

Kate and Rebecca sit in the window seat of the Bennets' front room.

"But does your aunt not realize that once you have been vaccinated, your chance of getting the disease is greatly reduced?" Kate says.

"Aunt Clara is not willing to take even a remote chance, I am afraid. She feels her brother would never forgive her if I stayed in Victoria and then came down with smallpox. She is insistent I leave on the next steamship with one of her housemaids. Since the disease is rampant in San Francisco, we will only stay long enough to disembark on one boat and board another for New York."

"How can I bear my life without you?" Kate is as distraught as she has ever been.

Rebecca grabs Kate's hands. "You are my one and only kindred spirit, Kate, and I will miss you so desperately. I promise I will write to you daily. Or, if I figure out a way, I will send telegrams and have them mailed from San Francisco."

"I can imagine part of you is filled with exhilaration at the thought of being reunited with Jeremiah Fortune."

"I cannot lie, the thought has crossed my mind." Rebecca picks up the teapot and fills Kate's cup. "But I expected another letter from him by now."

"Nothing has come, I'm afraid."

"Perhaps unraveling his marriage is more involved than he realized."

Kate nods, takes a sip of tea.

"And what news of Mr. O'Brien?" Rebecca asks.

"He left for New Westminster on business, but I wonder if his real reason is to escape the epidemic. He asked me to join him. Said he would bring along his head maid as a chaperone."

"How could you resist such an offer?" Rebecca says, jokingly.

"Quite easily, as it turns out. But what Mr. Eamonn O'Brien may not realize is that just days ago, the smallpox virus was carried to the mainland aboard the steamship *Otter*, and will be there to greet him when he disembarks."

"Sounds like there is no escaping this disease."

Kate looks at her friend and tears well in her eyes. "I will miss you so, Rebecca."

"Oh, my dearest friend." Rebecca wraps her arms around Kate and holds her close.

Kate arrives home to voices in the kitchen. Lucy stands with Old Pierre at the back door, while Mrs. Fleming translates for Mama.

"I was told that Indians employed in Victoria were not required to leave," Mama says.

"Old Pierre wishes Lucy to join her family on Discovery Island," Mrs. Fleming says. "The quarantine is for her safety and for the safety of the whole community."

"William would have made sure Lucy was vaccinated, Flora, so there should be no concern for safety."

"Lucy, you *have* been vaccinated, have you not?" Kate says.

Lucy nods, but Kate is unsure.

"When are they to leave?" Mama asks.

Mrs. Fleming asks Old Pierre. "He says they will leave by week's end."

Lucy says something to Old Pierre in a pleading tone. He speaks to her firmly but without a raised voice.

"Lucy was just off for several days, gathering plants and

what not, and now this?" Mama says. "How am I to wait out a plague without a housemaid, for goodness knows how long?" She shakes her head and leaves the kitchen.

Lucy follows Old Pierre out the back door, carrying a basket of clean laundry to hang on the line. She pleads with him again, but he shakes his head without saying another word.

"Lucy wants to stay here but her father says no," Mrs. Fleming says, as they watch Old Pierre head down the path by the barn. "He is right to insist she joins her family on Discovery Island. I so worry for all the Indians on this island." She gathers her shawl and handbag. "I will speak to your mama. Perhaps I can find some temporary help."

"Thank you, Mrs. Fleming. You are a good friend to us." Kate says. As Mrs. Fleming walks out of the kitchen to find Mama, Kate goes out the back door.

"Lucy, you must be honest with me," she says as she grabs one end of a sheet and secures it to the clothesline. "Were you vaccinated or not?"

"Yes, here." Lucy points to her upper arm. "Scab on my arm. At reserve."

On the Wharf Street pier, several workmen load trunks and crates onto the steamship. Kate's arms are tightly wrapped around Rebecca. Neither wants to let go. While Mrs. Bennet gives her housemaid last orders, Mr. Bennet checks his pocket watch.

"It is time to board, Rebecca," he says.

Rebecca releases the embrace. Tears well in her round brown eyes. "We will see one another again, Kate, I am most sure of that."

"I will cling to that hope." After all the devastating events of the past weeks, Kate feels numb. Even to Rebecca's tears.

Rebecca kisses Kate's cheek and says her goodbyes to Mr. and Mrs. Bennet, as she and the housemaid walk the wooden plank onto the boat. A horn sounds as the paddlewheels spin, churning up the water. Kate and Rebecca wave frantically to one another as the steamer pulls away from the pier. Kate has been given a delicious taste of what it's like to have a loving friendship, a kindred spirit, as Rebecca calls it. As the steamer cruises farther and farther out into the harbor, she knows she may never see Rebecca again. Arthur's face unexpectedly pops into her mind. Another person she loves that she may never see again.

As she gazes into shop windows along Government Street, she sees only fuzzy shapes; nothing is in focus. People float by like ghosts, neighing horses and children's laughter sound muted. She is startled when Hugh suddenly steps in front of her, wearing his smart blue uniform and looking as handsome as ever. The misery has crept into her heart as well—it barely quickens at the sight of him.

"May I walk with you?" he asks.

She nods and continues down the plank walkway. He tips his hat to two older women who pass by.

He looks down at her left hand. "You are not wearing your engagement ring?" It has been almost a month since she wrote him to tell of her engagement to Mr. O'Brien.

"It is much too ostentatious."

"That grand, is it?" he says, deflated.

"The ring does not represent who I am."

"And who are you, Kate?"

"I wish I knew."

He stops and takes both her hands in his. Looks deep into her eyes. "Break off the engagement."

"It is too late."

"It is never too late," he says. "I cannot claim to be able to match O'Brien's fortune, but in two years, I will inherit enough for us and your family to live comfortably."

"In two years, we will have lost everything." Kate slips

her hands out of his. "O'Brien has already given promissory notes to Papa's creditors."

Hugh looks away, dejected. They continue walking in silence.

"Is it true that the HMS *Forward* has been commissioned to force the tribes in the Northerners' Encampment back to their home villages?" Kate has been stewing on this since she overheard Mr. Trutch and Mr. Pemberton at the engagement party. Hugh would surely not support such action.

"Would you rather the disease remains in Victoria to fester and spread?" he says.

"But don't you see?" A deep ache simmers. "Smallpox will be carried back to their home villages up and down the coast. It will mean certain death for entire Indian populations."

"I have heard many officials in town say that it would not be the worst thing to happen. Natives cause a world of trouble for the colony. Besides, they are less ... human than you and I."

Kate stops walking. She's shocked and sickened to hear those words come out of Hugh's mouth.

"Less human? Are those really your words, or are you just repeating what you have been told?"

He sighs, looks into the distance. "I do feel pity for the natives."

"Pity is a shallow emotion. It allows you to look on from a distance at the suffering of others."

"But don't you see, Kate? My job is to protect and defend Britain's interests and her people from whatever threats may come. And this includes the very real threat of the many Indian tribes who are carrying this deadly disease."

"I would say that the Royal Navy is the true threat here." Kate is seething mad as she crosses the dusty road.

"Kate, wait ..."

She turns to Hugh. "How could I have ever thought what I felt for you was love?"

Hugh looks shattered.

As she walks away, she remains numb. She is almost sure that this is the last conversation she will ever have with Hugh.

It first sounded like a meowing cat, but as Kate gets closer to the house, she can hear it is Mama weeping. Another of her melancholic spells? If so, Kate is sure she cannot endure it today. She walks up the steps, rests her forehead on the cool wooden door for a long moment before she opens it. Mama's piercing cries send a chill up Kate's back. Lucy, with tears running down her face, rushes down the hallway carrying towels and cloths.

“Lucy, what is it?” Kate asks.

Looking straight through Kate, she scrambles up the stairs. Kate follows her into James’s room. There he lies, moaning, face red as a radish. His eyes are vacant.

# Chapter 20

Mama anxiously paces the room while Lucy sits on the bed, wiping James's face and her own tears, with a cloth.

"Lucy ... Lucy ..." James calls out weakly in his stupor, holding out his hand for her to take, which she does.

This cannot be happening, Kate thinks, as she caresses James's sweaty head, burning with fever. It was mid-March, six weeks ago, since the Brother Jonathan docked with the first smallpox patient. She had hoped with all her heart that her family would miraculously be immune from the disease. But Papa warned her that one in fifty people may contract the virus even though they have been inoculated. But why did her brother have to be among that small number?

The gloom that first settled into her day has become a darker, more sinister demon.

Mama flops on a chair in the corner of the room, hands covering her face. Papa listens to James's chest with the stethoscope. Feels for his pulse. He opens James's mouth. Small red spots cover his tongue.

"Papa?" Kate says. "What can be done?"

He removes the stethoscope and stands, looking defeated. "We can keep him comfortable and pray to God he recovers."

"Stay ... stay with me." James looks up at Lucy. She holds his hand tighter.

Kate finds Papa in his study, puffing on his pipe, staring out the window at Nora, grazing in the field lit orange by the setting sun.

"How is Mama?"

He slowly swivels in his chair to face Kate. "She is, of course, distraught. I gave her some brandy to help her sleep."

Papa went for days with very little sleep when the smallpox epidemic erupted, vaccinating both townsfolk and Indians alike.

"What about the other Indian tribes? How are they faring?" she asks.

"Some natives have immunity because of the outbreak that occurred decades ago. Others do not, I'm afraid. And some on the reserve, in the encampments, or even those in town who have been immunized, will still succumb to the disease."

"What's being done?"

"Two rough buildings have been constructed as a smallpox hospital in the Northerners' Encampment. Reverend Garrett has taken the lead to care for the sick and dying."

"I want to help, Papa."

"Florence Nightingale herself would not be able to bring solace to those poor souls."

"Still. Take me with you when you go. I am sure I can be of some assistance."

"Lucy leaves tomorrow for Discovery Island. I am afraid that with the epidemic spreading, I cannot be here to care for James. It will land on your shoulders, Kitty. Your mama is in no frame of mind to do so."

"James will not allow Lucy to leave his side," Kate says.

"He has no choice."

"But she is the only one he asks for. What if his recovery depends on her?"

Papa sighs, rubs his forehead.

"Are you afraid, Papa?"

"As afraid as I have ever been in my entire life."

Papa, always the one caring for others, and very rarely receiving comfort in return. Kate wraps her arms around him.

A loon call wakes Kate with a start. A dream. Must have been. She finds herself curled up in a chair in James's room. The blaze in the fireplace has burned down, casting only glimmering light now. Lucy sits on the bed, quietly singing as she wrings out a cloth and gently wipes James's bare chest and arms. Kate goes to James. Tiny red flecks are now visible on his face, arms, and hands. She lifts the sheet and sees it has not yet spread to his legs and feet. However, his face is still burning with fever.

Kate holds out her hand for the cloth. "Sleep now, Lucy. I will take over."

Lucy looks exhausted but shakes her head. "No, I stay," and resumes singing.

Old Pierre waits outside the kitchen door. Lucy's expression is pure anguish as she wraps a shawl around her shoulders.

"This is for the best, Lucy. For you and for your whole village," Kate says. Lucy opens the door and leaves without a word, following several paces behind her father.

After checking on James, who is sleeping as comfortably as he can, Kate goes to her room and sits at her desk. Out the window she sees Songish canoes, swarming like a school of spawning salmon, from the mouth of the harbor. Kate desperately hopes the quarantine will save the Songish people, unlike the poor Tsimshian, Haida, and other tribes that are quickly being annihilated. A jab stabs at her chest.

James fades in and out of delirium. The disease gives off a stench of rotting flesh, which Kate knows she must get used to. As she changes the sheet beneath him, she sees the red bumps have spread to his legs and feet. Mama stands at the door, too grief-stricken to enter.

"Lucy, are you there?" James calls out. "Orca ... ride on its back ... under water ... sea wolf."

"I am here, James," Kate says, pulling a sheet over his shivering body. She prays James's spirit helper is not here to guide him into the next life.

James breaks down in tears. "Where have you gone?"

"Be calm. Lucy will be back soon."

"Did she promise? Tell me she promised."

Kate stifles a sob, nods. But it doesn't stop James from continuing to call out for Lucy. Footsteps race up the stairs. Papa, still wearing his coat, places his doctor's bag on the floor and wraps Mama in a comforting embrace, before she turns and leaves for her room.

"How is he?" Papa says. He throws off his coat and opens his bag.

Kate lifts the sheet to show him the rash on James's lower body. "Other than this, he is much the same."

Papa takes a vial out of his bag and lifts James's head.

"Is that laudanum?" she asks.

"Yes, Kitty." James winces and shakes his head back and forth when the sedative is emptied into his mouth. "This should help with his agitation." Papa checks James's eyes and his pulse.

"Where were you today, Papa?"

"At the encampment hospital. Six Indians arrive each day and almost as many are buried." He pulls the stethoscope out of his bag to listen to James's chest. "Reverend Garrett, already heavily burdened, has had to add coffin maker and gravedigger to his duties."

There's a tapping at the front door. It soon turns to pounding. Papa and Kate share a look.

Kate hurries down the stairs and opens the front door to find Lucy, soaked to the skin and shivering.

"Lucy? What happened? Why are you here?"

Lucy hides her eyes behind clumps of dripping wet hair, stares at the ground. Her arms are wrapped around her shivering body.

"Come in before you catch your death." Kate guides her in and closes the door behind her.

"James?" She looks up anxiously.

"He is resting."

Lucy starts up the stairs but Kate stops her.

"You can see him soon enough. Go into the kitchen and warm yourself by the stove. I will bring you dry clothes."

Reluctantly, Lucy sloshes down the hallway toward the kitchen, leaving a damp trail behind her. Did she climb out of the canoe and make her way to shore? She must have. Kate hurries up the stairs to find her some clothes.

Lucy sits by the stove, holding a hot cup of tea and wearing a skirt and blouse of Kate's. Mama paces the room while Papa and Kate sit next to Lucy.

"Does your papa know where you are?" Kate asks.

Lucy nods.

"I presume you came back to care for James?" Papa says.

Lucy nods, tears spill down her tormented face. "Did I make James's smallpox?"

"A few other children in James's school have also become ill," Papa says. "He could have easily contracted the virus from one of them."

Lucy's body rocks forward and back, cries out with relief. Both Kate and Papa are surprised when it is Mama who puts a calming hand on Lucy's shoulder.

# Chapter 21

Scribbles on notepaper and open medical textbooks are scattered around Kate's bed and desk. Although she has taken meticulous notes on smallpox, hoping she can find even one new piece of information, she has learned nothing more than what Papa has already told her. She clears her desk of the notebooks and takes a sheet of writing paper from her drawer.

*26 May 1862*

*Dearest Arthur,*

*By now you will have received Mama's letter informing you that James has come down with smallpox. I am now tasked to carry on her story.*

*I am convinced this disease was sent directly from the devil himself. I combed through my medical textbooks for answers, but I found no cure or new treatment for this horrible scourge. Papa sedated James as much as his small body would allow, but the high fevers, pain, and agitation set James screaming in agony both day and night. It began as a rash on his entire body and turned into pus-filled abscesses. There was so little we could do to comfort him. Lucy, our housemaid, who was supposed to be quarantined on Discovery Island with the rest of the Songish reserve, has barely left James's side since the moment he became ill. When either Mama or I try to relieve Lucy, James calls out for her alone, and is agitated until she returns to his bedside. All this said, I am happy to report that James is over the worst of the disease, and Papa feels he will make a full recovery, although the smallpox will scar his delicate skin for life as a brutal reminder. It is my belief that Lucy made the difference in our brother's living through the disease. Even Mama is treating*

*Lucy with more warmth and respect. I'm witnessing a very different side of Mama and liking this new woman more and more each day.*

*I am deeply troubled about the northern Indians camped in and around Victoria. Smallpox has spread through every tribe. Papa visited the Haida village at Ogden Point and found it all but abandoned. Their lodges were left open, guns, blankets, dresses, and trinkets scattered everywhere. Under the floorboards were the bodies of men, women, and children who had fallen to the disease. The small hospital built on the Northerners' Encampment, for the natives suffering with the disease, is full to overflowing with many deaths daily. There are not enough hands to care for the sick and dying, or to bury the dead. Earlier this month, naval ships (my Lieutenant Ashton is complicit in this atrocity) "escorted" over twenty Indian canoes out of the harbor to carry the disease to their home villages. At the end of April, nearly all of the Tsimshian had left, torching their dwellings as they departed. The police also evicted Stikines from their camps, and destroyed all lodges at the Haida camp, leaving 200 people without homes or canoes.* The Daily British Colonist *newspaper recently reported that while politicians and townspeople were celebrating Queen Victoria's birthday (only two days ago), on the beach within sight of the legislature buildings, three Indians lay dead. Am I the only one to see this as a tragic irony? The newspaper estimates that at least one-third of the northern tribes have died already. At this present rate of mortality, I fear whole races of Indians will die out before too long.*

*On another note, although Mr. O'Brien has negotiated with Papa's creditors and there is no longer any financial urgency, Mama is still insisting a date be set for the wedding. Oh, Arthur, it is a day I anticipate with pure dread. I do not mean to sound like a martyr—I am resolute about my decision—but you are one of the only people I can share my honest feelings with. However, what will bring me much happiness when I become Mrs. Eamonn O'Brien is that I will be your patron, so you are able to live in Paris and devote all your time to your art.*

*I miss you so very much, my dear brother. Although I have photographs of you, I pray with all my heart that one day I will be able to see you in person.*

*Sending my deepest love,*

*K*

Kate can hear voices, laughs, and clinking glasses from the drawing room downstairs. She takes one more look in her bedroom mirror at the blue satin brocade gown that Mama had made in San Francisco, along with several other new dresses. Now that money is no longer an immediate concern, Mama has been spending more freely. But why does she feel it is fitting to throw a games party just because Mr. O'Brien is back in Victoria? The Harding family has become nothing more than beggars with palms outstretched to this man.

Kate walks by James's bedroom and peers through the door. James is propped up on his bed with pillows. Lucy, as always, is at his side. Almost all of his crusty white scabs have fallen off, which means soon he will no longer be contagious and will be able to leave the house. His eyes are bright, and his curious mind is as active as ever.

"When you die, Lucy, which animal do you wish to become?"

"My grandmother says raven. I have trickster spirit."

"Like the time you hid all my toys around the house and made a game of me finding them?"

Lucy nods, laughs.

"I wish to change into a bear or a killer whale. Or maybe even an owl."

"Owl is full of magic."

"What kind of magic?"

"Enough talk, more eating. I made fish broth that you like. Will make you strong."

"I am already strong, Lucy. See?" James flexes his bicep that is as skinny as a new shoot.

"Yes, very strong. I must leave, back to the kitchen. Help with the party."

Lucy meets Kate in the hallway. Her eyes immediately fix on the pearl necklace Kate is wearing.

"Pretty," she says before she heads down the stairs.

"Why are you not at the party, Kate?" James asks as Kate enters his room.

"Because I would far rather be here with you." She sits on the side of his bed, blue silk fanning around her.

James rubs his finger over the sapphire engagement ring Mama insisted she wear. "When you marry Mr. O'Brien, will you move far away?"

"I will never be far from you." Kate stands, kisses his head of brown curls, and tucks him in. "I best go greet our guests. Lucy will be up later to check on you."

Kate breathes deeply before she enters the drawing room, to see the games have already begun. The one in progress is obviously "Lookabout." The Flemings, the Trutches, the Pembertons, the Finlaysons, the Bennets, Mama and Papa are seated, while Mr. O'Brien, already weaving under the weight of his whiskey, looks around the room—on top of tables, shelves, behind paintings, under chairs, while everyone else is entertained, watching him search.

"Ah ha!" O'Brien says and picks up an old key from behind a book on the shelf and shows it around. "At last."

Claps from the other guests.

"I will not be hiring you for detective work, O'Brien,"

Mr. Pemberton says, chuckling. "You can be sure of that."

"Now a game of 'Charades,'" Mama says, holding one of Papa's top hats filled with small pieces of paper. "Flora, how about you go first?"

Mrs. Fleming reaches into the hat and pulls out her prompt to act out. She kneels down and makes a scooping action.

"She's digging something," says Mrs. Trutch.

"Surely she is searching for gold," Mr. Bennet calls out.

"Or tunneling to China," O'Brien says, laughing too loudly at his own joke.

Mrs. Fleming draws a straight line with her imaginary shovel. Pinches her thumb and forefinger and gestures she is placing something in the row.

"Planting a garden," Kate says.

"That is it," Mrs. Fleming says with a smile. "Your turn, Katherine."

Kate reaches into the hat for her prompt. It reads: *Your wedding day*. Did Mama plan this one just for her? Kate pretends to look into a mirror as she dresses.

"She's preparing herself for some occasion," Mrs. Finlayson says.

Kate continues her pantomime, twirling her hair in a fancy style, placing a veil over her head.

"By the somber look on her face, I am sure she is dressing for a funeral," Mr. Trutch says.

Kate points to her engagement ring.

"You are dressing for your husband's funeral," Mrs. Trutch says.

Kate can't contain herself and bursts out laughing. Everyone smiles but looks puzzled.

After "Charades," the group plays "Pass the Slipper" and "Forfeits." Kate is relieved when the guests finally get ready to leave.

O'Brien puts down his glass and stands. He holds onto a table, then the wall to steady himself as he leaves the room, probably gone to relieve himself of all the whiskey he's consumed. After seeing some guests to the door, Kate begins collecting empty glasses and dishes and placing them onto a tray.

When she enters the kitchen, she almost drops the tray.

Lucy stands behind O'Brien holding a large kitchen knife to his throat. Kate sees that Lucy's blouse has been torn down the front. Kate tries to say something, but no words come out of her mouth.

"I killed a man and would do the same to you!" Lucy has a frenzied look on her face. The steel from the knife glints in the light of the lantern.

"Come, squaw, I am sure you are used to submitting to men's advances," O'Brien slurs nonchalantly, even with a knife about to slice his artery.

Kate finally finds her voice. "Put the knife down, Lucy." She places the tray from her shaking hands onto the table. "Leave him be."

"Your squaw is threatening me with a lethal weapon. Fortunately, the Superintendent of Police happens to be in the next room."

"And I will tell Mr. Pemberton you assaulted our housemaid."

Lucy continues pressing the knife into the flesh on O'Brien's neck.

Kate walks slowly toward Lucy, holding out her hand. "Hand me the knife, Lucy."

After several moments, Lucy finally loosens her hold around O'Brien. Kate takes the knife from her hand and puts it in a drawer. Lucy wraps the torn blouse around herself; her body begins to shake.

"Leave at once, Mr. O'Brien." Kate takes off the engagement ring and slams it on the table beside her. "And I will make sure you never set foot in this house again."

"Much too late for that, Katherine." O'Brien smirks. "I

practically own this house." He glances down at the ring on the table. Tries to touch her face. She bats his hand away and he staggers out of the kitchen. A queasy ache hits Kate right in the stomach.

Lucy is still trembling. Her face is flushed and covered in a film of sweat from the ordeal.

"He won't hurt you now," Kate says.

"I told truth. I did kill a man," Lucy says, her dark eyes searching Kate's face for reproach. When there is none, Lucy sinks into a chair, covers herself with crossed arms, and starts to cry. Kate sits next to her.

"Long ago, before aunty move to brothel, we walk to the reserve from town. Sun was almost down behind hills. A man with too much drink in him came toward us on the road. He wears fancy clothes, a pack on his back. Said he is a miner. Struck it big in the gold fields. Patted his fat pack. Said bad things to aunty, grabbed her hair, pulled her into bushes. She screaming. On the ground, he on top of her. I find a heavy wood board, strike at his head many times. Nails from the board here and here." Lucy points to a few spots on the back of her head. "He bleed and bleed. Then was dead."

Kate nods. She's shocked at Lucy's murderous tale, but also horrified at how Indian women are so brazenly denigrated.

"Your story can never leave this kitchen. Do you understand, Lucy?"

"That's not all," Lucy says. Her body hasn't stopped shaking. "I took his pack. Full of treasure."

Mama comes into the kitchen. "Katherine, do you know why Mr. O'Brien left so abruptly?"

Lucy slumps off her chair onto the floor.

# Chapter 22

It's late into the night. Two candles cast a dim light, as Kate sits in silence at the dining room table with Papa and Mama, who are lost in their own thoughts.

Finally, Mama speaks up. "Perhaps you misinterpreted what happened, Katherine. What one sees can at times be deceiving."

"How can you say that, Mama? Lucy's blouse was ripped away. Mr. O'Brien's immoral intentions were most clear," Kate says in a firm tone. "We must sever all ties with this despicable man, no matter what the consequences are."

"I have to agree with Kitty on this matter, Louisa. O'Brien's own hasty exit is an admission of his guilt."

Mama is pale and her expression somber. This night will change all of their lives.

"I will speak with Reverend Garrett to see if there is a bed for Lucy at the hospital," Papa says.

"But Papa, are you sure Lucy is not just traumatized? She endured a very distressing incident this evening."

"I am most sure it is more than trauma, Kitty. You helped me examine her. She has all the early symptoms of the virus—fever, chills, and severe pain in her head."

Deep down, Kate knows this, but she doesn't want to face the horror. Physicians must face the facts, not surrender to emotion or false hopes.

"Lucy would have been given scab to arm inoculation on the reserve. It is not as effective," Papa says.

"But why didn't we see these signs before this evening?" Kate says. She blames herself for being buried in her own self-pity, rather than looking more clearly at what has been happening around her. First with James and now with Lucy.

Papa shakes his head and looks down at his hands, resting on the table.

"We will not send Lucy to the hospital," Mama says.

"What are you saying, Louisa? Surely we cannot send her to Discovery Island to infect others."

"We will care for her in our home," Mama is calm and matter of fact. "At least until the bank evicts us."

Papa looks as surprised by Mama's statement as Kate is.

"I don't think that is a wise decision, my dear. I worry

about how an extra burden would compromise your own health. You and Kitty will have more than enough to do, running this household now that we are without a housemaid."

"Lucy was unwavering in her care and affection for James," Mama says. "I am not sure he would have survived the vile disease without her, William. She had a chance to save herself and instead chose to be at our son's side, morning and night. I will not have her suffer on her own among strangers."

"She is right, Papa. And I am sure Mrs. Fleming will help out when needed."

Kate has finally witnessed a crack in Mama's rock-solid façade that has kept the best parts of her hidden and closely guarded for as long as she can remember. She is astonished that Lucy is the one to be credited with crumbling the armor around Mama's heart.

"I guess it is decided, then. I will do my best to provide whatever she needs to make her comfortable." Papa stands. "Starting this very minute."

"You two go to Lucy," Mama says. "I will clean up after the party."

Lucy is curled up in bed in the maid's room. Her whole

body shakes with chills. Her chattering teeth interrupt her quiet singing. Kate takes her hand while Papa examines inside her mouth, feels for her pulse.

"Cool cloth on her head, Kitty."

Kate pulls a cloth out of a bowl filled with water, wrings it out, and places it on Lucy's forehead. She knows this is only the very beginning of the agony to come.

The late June sun is warm on her back, as Kate crunches through the beach pebbles by Laurel Point. Mrs. Fleming insisted Kate take some time for herself this morning, after days on end where she barely stepped outside of the house, even for a breath of fresh air. The harbor is bare of Indian canoes that usually crisscross the water. All that is left are steamers, and only a few of Her Majesty's warships at anchor, including the HMS *Forward*. Any romantic thoughts and feelings for Hugh have all but vanished. He was in full support of his mission to escort scores of Indians, carrying the smallpox virus on their clothes, blankets, and inside their bodies, back to their home villages. And there is no doubt he knows this meant certain annihilation.

Kate sits on a log, opens an envelope with a Sacramento, California, postmark, and pulls out the note.

**_Western Union Telegraph Company_**

New York City, June 4, 1862

*My dearest Kate,*

*On the steamer to San Francisco, I made friends with Mrs. Serrano from California, who agreed to mail my telegrams to Victoria.*

*As I have such little space to write, I have to tell you in only a few words that all my hopes and dreams have collapsed into a heap of ruin. When Jeremiah went back to St. Lucia to divorce his wife, it turns out he instead reconciled with her. But not only that, she is also now carrying his child. I am distraught beyond comprehension, and the only person who can console me is you, dear Kate. Papa has agreed to pay your passage to New York, and you are welcome to stay in our home as long as you are able. Forever would be most preferable. Aunt Clara has wanted to visit New York for some time, so she could be your travel companion. Please say you'll come, Kate. Mail a note to Mrs.*

*Serrano and she will send me a telegram with your answer.*

*Your loving kindred spirit,*

*Rebecca*

Kate has been taking turns with Mama and Mrs. Fleming, tending to the needs of the household, as well as nursing Lucy in her worsening condition. They have also both had to coax James back to good health and comfort him, since his beloved Lucy fell ill. And now this request from Rebecca. But she knows how she must answer Rebecca during this desperate time. Soon her family will be forced to sell even more of their belongings and pack up their home. Now she wishes she had sold her engagement ring to Mr. Bedwell, the jeweler, rather than sending it back to Mr. O'Brien. It was worth enough to hold off their creditors for at least a month.

Kate takes a longer walk home by Shoal Point. As gentle waves lap on the shore and seagulls wail overhead, thoughts spin around Kate's head. What she desires most is to comfort Rebecca during her trying predicament, and to meet Dr. Elizabeth Blackwell. Both are in New York City. But these are two more dreams she must let go of.

Ahead on the beach, a native woman holds a baby, while

a young boy with a shovel digs a hole—Haidas who stayed behind to care for the sick and dying. The woman's face is dark, fine lines carving out her shock and devastation. A blanket covers her head and most of her body, including her skirt that is soiled with sand. As Kate gets closer, the stench of rotting flesh nauseates her. She breathes deeply several times to overcome the queasiness, and ties her scarf over her face. What she thought was a log is the body of a man, maybe the woman's husband, clearly ravaged by smallpox. The woman says something to the boy and then holds out the baby to Kate. She takes the baby while they struggle to lift the man's body into the grave.

Kate looks into the tiny face covered in scabs. When she realizes the baby is also dead, she fights to catch her breath. First tears flow, and then all her grief and loss that she had buried until now pours out in heaving sobs. In the face of this baby, she sees her dead infant siblings, James, who came close to death, and now Lucy, Arthur, whom she may never see again, and Rebecca and Hugh, two people she loves and has lost forever. She also sees herself, crushed by the great loss of her dream of becoming a doctor.

The woman and boy watch as Kate slumps to the ground, rocking the baby, crying and moaning. After several minutes, the woman takes the baby from her and gently places it in the grave beside the man. With her bare hands, Kate helps them cover the bodies with cold, damp sand and gravel, until they are fully buried. But when the tide comes in, the forceful waves, like workman's hands, will pull the bodies out into the ocean. The woman bows her head to Kate in gratitude, as she and the boy walk back down the beach, leaving Kate crushed, weeping.

When Kate arrives back, the house is quiet. She takes off her sandy boots and goes up the stairs directly to Lucy's room. Mrs. Fleming stands by the bed, while Papa listens to Lucy's chest with his stethoscope. Lucy lies still, covered in angry red abscesses.

"Papa?"

The grave look on his face tells the story. "I'm afraid it won't be long now."

Kate was sure she had no more tears to cry, but more stream down her face.

"I have sent word to Old Pierre on Discovery Island," Mrs. Fleming says.

"Where's Mama?"

"She took James to the shops in town," Mrs. Fleming says. "He had to be peeled away from Lucy's side."

"You go home, Mrs. Fleming," Kate says, wiping her face with her sleeve. "I am here now."

"I cleared my calendar of engagements this whole week. I will come by again first thing in the morning."

"You have been unfaltering in your friendship," Papa says, putting the stethoscope back in his black doctor's bag. "Indeed, we are so very grateful to you, Mrs. Fleming."

She smiles weakly, picks up her bag. "Until the morning." Mrs. Fleming leaves the room.

The light in Lucy's room is now dim, as the late-day sun drops in the sky. Kate looks out the window to see Nora grazing in the field.

"I saw a turtle in the pond today, with yellow stripes on his head and legs, sunning himself on a nice log," James says to Lucy. He insisted on taking over from Kate, gently patting Lucy's face with the damp cloth. Lucy lays listless, eyes closed, slowly sinking into her permanent sleep before death. She is so still, Kate takes her hand and feels for her pulse. It is still there but weak and irregular.

"James, it's your bedtime," Kate says.

"But I want to tell Lucy about the sweets Mrs. Parker gave me in town today."

"You can tell her tomorrow." Kate goes to the door, holds out her hand for James to take. "Come." But before he does, he gently strokes Lucy's hair and then rests his cheek on her head. This gesture of love and compassion threatens to break Kate right open.

Kate helps James undress in his bedroom.

"I asked Lucy if she was going to die," he says, pulling on his nightshirt.

Kate has kept putting off this difficult conversation with him. And here he's the one to take the lead.

"And what was her answer?"

"She told me her body will die, but she will live on. Do you believe that, Kate?"

"I am not sure what I believe."

"Lucy said she would always be close to me, even if I can't see her or touch her. What do you think she means, Kate?"

Kate gathers her thoughts. "When I care very deeply for someone, I feel they are close to me, as if I've made a space for them in my heart. Like our brother, Arthur, whom you have never met." And Rebecca, Kate thinks, and even Hugh.

James feels his chest for his beating heart.

She kisses the scars on James's forehead and pulls up his covers.

Kate sits at her desk. She has procrastinated long enough. Dips her pen into the inkwell.

*23 June '61*

*My dearest Rebecca,*

*It is with a deep sadness that I write to you. I was so desperately sorry to hear of Mr. Fortune's change of heart, and how this decision must have pierced the depths of your soul. All that you wished for has been so cruelly and unexpectedly snatched away.*

*If there were any way I could board the next ship sailing to New York City to comfort you during this difficult time, I would do so in a heartbeat. But, alas, I am unable to leave my family, with so many burdens I cannot even begin to describe in this short note. But know that you will always be in my thoughts, and especially in my heart.*

*Your loving friend,*

*Kate*

The lantern casts eerie shadows down the black hallway as Kate makes her way to Lucy's room. Lucy's eyes are narrow slits. She still gasps for every breath.

Kate places the lantern down and picks up a cup of water for Lucy to sip, but she shakes her head.

"Did you hear?" Lucy asks in a whisper.

"Hear what, Lucy?"

"Loon. Been calling you."

Kate places her hand on Lucy's head of black hair. She's obviously in a laudanum haze. She checks the sores on Lucy's face and arms. Some have already crusted over. Kate wishes she would cling to life just a while longer, until the worst of this disease is over.

"Medicine ... power," Lucy whispers. "Not from books ... Inside you."

Lucy's words burn right through the deepest longing in Kate's soul. Even if she does have medicine power, as Lucy calls it, it is forever out of her grasp.

Lucy's eyes close, her breath becomes raspy and shallow. She will not live out the night.

# Chapter 23

Empty boxes are scattered around Kate's bedroom. She searches under her bed for the medical textbooks in their hiding place—*The Diseases of Women with Child and in Child Bearing* and *The Syllabus of Lectures on Midwifery.* Since she no longer has use for these, she will sell them back to Mr. Vogel, if he will take them. She is surprised how dispassionate she feels, as she flips through the pages before placing them into a sack. Papa's book by Dr. Gray—*Anatomy: Descriptive and Surgical*— has also collected a layer of dust under her bed. She must be sure to slip this book into a box packed with Papa's other texts.

Her desk is stacked with notebooks, filled with her scribbles about anatomy, diseases, treatments, and medicines. To what purpose did she spend those many hours of her life studying? Mama was right all along. Her time would have been much better spent mastering needlepoint, sewing, or playing the piano. The more useful pursuits for women.

Although the full summer heat has filled every inch of the house, Kate stacks wood in her fireplace. Places the notebooks from her desk onto the hearth. She reads through the top one, filled with detailed anatomy recordings—the layers of muscles and ligaments, veins and arteries, the chambers and mechanisms of the heart, and the hundreds of bones in the human skeleton. She rips out the first page, sets it on fire and places it inside the piled wood. Once the paper has caught fire, she throws in the entire notebook. As she adds another notebook, there's a knock on her door.

It's Maisie, their new housemaid. A hefty girl from a cattle farm in the Highlands of Scotland. Even in their dire financial straits, Mama could not live long without a housemaid, and Papa had no choice but to agree.

Maisie looks curiously at the fire, now making the room stifling. "Mrs. Fleming is here to see you, Miss Kate. She comes with a ... gentleman." Her large gray eyes and raised bushy eyebrows give her an expression of permanent surprise.

Which gentleman could that be? Kate had overheard Mama and Mrs. Fleming talk of eligible men in town as potential suitors for her. Would Mrs. Fleming be so bold as to bring one around uninvited?

"Tell her I will be down shortly."

The flames gobble up her notebook.

Mrs. Fleming and the mysterious man are nowhere to be found. Where could Maisie have taken them?

When she enters the kitchen, Mrs. Fleming and Old Pierre stand at the back door. He is holding the jewelry box that she gave to Lucy.

"Katherine," Mrs. Fleming says. "Old Pierre would like to give this to you."

He hands Kate the box.

Mrs. Fleming continues. "Before the quarantine on Discovery Island, Lucy told her papa that she had planned to give the jewelry box to you."

Lucy must have wanted to give her all the jewelry she'd collected for her trousseau.

"Thank you. I will always treasure it with the fondest memories of Lucy."

Mrs. Fleming translates. He smiles, nods, and then speaks.

"He wants you to open the box," Mrs. Fleming says.

Kate opens the lid and the Mozart concerto plays slower and slower, rapidly fading out. Instead of jewelry, inside are two small leather pouches, which she holds up. Old Pierre keeps nodding and gesturing for her to unfasten the strings securing the top. The small sacks are filled with gold dust.

"What? How?" Kate is shocked and so is Mrs. Fleming. Old Pierre chuckles. "I ... I cannot take this," Kate says. This must be the treasure Lucy spoke of, taken from the miner who attacked Lucy's aunty. The miner Lucy killed.

"This is yours, Old Pierre. For your family," Kate says. She hands the pouches to him. He shakes his head and speaks to Mrs. Fleming.

"He says it was Lucy's wish for you to have the box and everything inside."

"What about Lucy's aunty? The one who lives ... in town? Surely she needs the money."

Mrs. Fleming asks Old Pierre.

"Lucy's aunty passed away," Mrs. Fleming says. "Poisoned with alcohol."

Kate takes this in. Wonders why Lucy didn't give her aunty the gold, since she was the victim.

"I don't know what to say," Kate says, still stunned as she pours a tiny sprinkle of gold dust into her hand. "Thank you so very much for your generosity, Old Pierre."

Old Pierre nods, opens the door, and waits for Mrs. Fleming outside.

"But, Mrs. Fleming, what am I to do?"

"My suggestion is to go directly to the Gold Exchange and, on your way there, give up a prayer of thanks to Lucy, Old Pierre, and the good Lord for the generous gift." She smiles, obviously excited for Kate, and joins Old Pierre down the path toward the barn.

Before she closes the box, Kate lifts out the two compartments. Beneath are two more bulging leather pouches. Surely, they must be filled with Lucy's jewelry. She opens one pouch and picks out a gold nugget the size of a large chestnut. She pours the contents of the pouches on the butcher's block, and many more nuggets of various sizes spill out. Kate cannot even comprehend the value of all this gold.

Kate excitedly paces the drawing room, while Papa and Mama sit down on the settee. She is anxious to erase the stress and trauma that have been etched on her parents' faces for months.

"What is it, Kitty?" Papa says.

Kate picks up a large envelope from the side table.

"I met with Mr. Bromley at the bank." She hands the envelope to Papa. "Open this."

Papa shares a curious look with Mama, as he opens the envelope and pulls out the papers.

"It is the deed to our house. Paid in full," Papa says, incredulous.

Mama holds her face between her hands in shock. "How on earth did you arrange this, Katherine? Did Mr. O'Brien come through with his promise?"

"Of course not, Mama. You have only Lucy to thank."

"Lucy?" Papa says.

"I cannot tell you the details of this gift, but Lucy provided us with enough money to pay off most of our debts. There is only one small loan left to pay."

Mama bursts out crying with relief, burying her face in Papa's shoulder. For fear of their disapproval, she doesn't tell her parents she also sent Arthur enough money to move to Paris and live comfortably, for a time, at least, while he pursues his art.

"I have something else to tell you," Kate says. "Rebecca Bennet has invited me to stay with her in New York City, and her father has kindly offered to pay my passage. With my entire being, I wish to accept."

The joy and relief of just a moment ago washes off both their faces. There is a long moment of uncomfortable silence.

"You cannot board a ship on your own for such a long journey. It would be most improper," Mama says.

"Mrs. Bennet has agreed to be my companion."

"Of course, we'd like to support you, Kitty," Papa says, "but you will still need some money and I'm afraid we have little to offer you."

"I will find work as a governess if I must, Papa. Please, I beg of you both to give me your blessing."

Mama and Papa search one another's faces for the answer.

"For all that you have done for this family," Papa says, "how could we refuse you?"

In her room, Kate kicks aside the empty boxes, pleased she was unhurried in her packing. She sees the stack of notebooks on the hearth she didn't get around to burning. She spins around her room, dancing, laughing. It feels as if a heavy packsack filled with boulders, that she has been carrying for months, has been lifted off her shoulders. And now she can breathe freely. A passage from *Jane Eyre* that she knows by heart comes to mind:

*I need not sell my soul to buy bliss. I have*

*an inward treasure born with me, which*
*can keep me alive if all extraneous delights*
*should be withheld or offered only at a price*
*I cannot afford to give.*

A knock on the door and Mama enters, holding up the emerald necklace and earrings.

"I am most sure Mr. Bedwell will pay top dollar for this exquisite set," Mama says.

"But I thought you sold the emeralds."

Mama sits on the bed, spreading out the jewelry. "I would like to tell you I kept the emeralds in case you needed the money. But to be truly honest, I clung to the notion that you needed to be Mr. O'Brien's bejeweled wife."

Kate sits with her on the bed. Mama takes Kate's hands and looks her right in the eyes.

"I now know you will never have to be any man's adornment."

# Chapter 24

On the Wharf Street pier, cows, pigs, and chickens are loaded into the lower deck of the steam ship *Commodore*, along with boxes of cargo and bags of mail. Kate watches as the workmen load her luggage and then her trunk, packed with her medical textbooks and notebooks. This is now real. Every cell of her body vibrates with excitement and anticipation.

People are milling about the pier, saying goodbye to their loved ones, including Mr. and Mrs. Bennet. Mama, Papa, James, and Sister Mary are here to see Kate off.

"Don't forget to send a note once you've landed in San Francisco," Mama says.

"Yes, Mama."

"And the moment you arrive in New York City."

"Of course, Mama."

"I do not know what I'll do without you, Kitty. May this journey bring you all your curious mind deserves."

"Thank you, Papa."

James runs into Kate's waiting arms. She picks him up and spins him around.

"Will you be gone forever, Kate?"

"I could never be away from you forever. I promise I will be back one day. In the meantime, I will write you letters, and you must write me back. Be a good boy for Mama, Papa, and Maisie."

She kisses his cheek and puts him down.

Kate takes Sister Mary's outstretched hands.

"You are now free to fulfill your purpose, Katherine."

"I am only but one step closer."

"First one step, and then another, and another. I am most certain you will find your way."

"Your friendship and guidance are what helped me believe it could be a possibility. And I will be forever grateful to you for that, Sister."

A raven circles overhead. It squawks, then makes a laughing sound before it soars away, high into the sky. Kate smiles. *Goodbye, Lucy.*

The steamship horn sounds. Mrs. Bennet says her last goodbyes and joins Kate on the gangway as they board the boat. As the steamer pulls away from the wharf, she imagines the HMS *Forward* at anchor in the Esquimalt harbor. A twinge grabs at her chest, but it soon fades.

She doesn't stand at the back of the boat with Mrs. Bennet and the many other passengers waving goodbye to loved ones on the shore. Instead, she walks straight to the front deck, as the steamer passes by all the places that hold so many memories.

# Acknowledgments

I am privileged to live and write on the unceded territory of the Lkwungen-speaking people of the Songhees and Esquimalt First Nations. From the Songhees First Nation, I wish to thank Florence Dick, Diane Sam, Mark Salter, and Christina Clarke for sharing with me their time, stories, wisdom, and blessings.

I am so grateful to have such a talented community of writing friends, who provided such thoughtful comments on early drafts of this book. Warm-hearted thanks to Diana Cranstoun, Diana Jones, and Shannon McFerran. I especially want to thank my dear friend, Tricia Dower, who painstakingly read and critiqued this novel, chapter by chapter. I so appreciate her insight into story and her incredible generosity.

Big thanks to my talented son, Joel Peterson, for creating such a perfect map for this novel. Thanks also to

Farrah Patterson and Aaron Florian for making the finishing touches to the map.

To my family and friends—your love and encouragement means the world to me.

Thanks to Peter Carver for his guiding hand in editing this book, and also to Richard Dionne, publisher of Red Deer Press.

Finally, here are the literary works referred to in the story, complete with their authors and the dates of their original publication:

"The Raven"—Edgar Allen Poe, 1845

*Vanity Fair*—William Makepeace Thackeray, 1847

*Jane Eyre*—Charlotte Brontë, 1847

"All Things Love Thee, So Do I"—Charles Horn, 1855

"She Walks in Beauty"—Lord Byron, 1814

# Historical Note

In *Wild Bird,* Kate Harding and her family sailed from London, England, in 1854 to Victoria's sleepy townsite of 500 immigrant settlers. They would have stepped ashore to find mostly open space, except for Fort Victoria's bastion and palisades, and very few other buildings. Beyond the townsite was mostly bush, some marshland, and Beacon Hill, teeming with deer, birds, and other wildlife. Further out was farmland, and across the Strait of Juan de Fuca, they would have seen snow-capped mountains in the Washington Territory.

Archeology tells us that Coast Salish people lived on the southern tip of Vancouver Island for thousands of years before Sir James Douglas established a Hudson's Bay fur trading post in 1842. Indigenous people were vital to the colony's economy and social fabric. Indigenous men assisted settlers in clearing land, building Fort Victoria in 1843, and unloading and loading cargo. And women, like Lucy, worked as domestic servants and sold food such as fish, seafood, and vegetables. Cheealthluc, the Songhees chief, appears in *Wild Bird*. Also known as King Freezy, he acted as a guide, translator, and key intermediary between the Songhees and the settlers.

As Victoria grew, so did tensions between the colonists and the Indigenous people. Colonists either pitied or felt revulsion toward First Nations' culture and living habits. I didn't want to sugar coat the racism of the time, so I included Joseph Trutch as a character in the novel. Trutch came to Victoria as a British surveyor in the 1850s, served as chief commissioner of lands and works, and later became a politician. Trutch was known for his racist views and his poor treatment of First Nations. The racism was not limited to townsfolk. From 1850–1870, it was routine practice for the Royal Navy, including Hugh Ashton's HMS *Forward*, to deploy warships against Indigenous people any time settlers were killed or ships attacked along the coast. This included the 1850 destruction of a Kwakwaka'wakw village on northern Vancouver Island.

In the spring of 1858, the steamer *Commodore* arrived from San Francisco, carrying 450 miners from countries all over the world, who were headed for the Fraser River gold fields. This nearly doubled Victoria's population. Miners had to first travel to Victoria to obtain a licence to prospect for gold, making Victoria the supply center for miners on their way to the Fraser River. With no hotels, miners had to pitch tents around the townsite. Over the months that followed, Victoria's population exploded to over 30,000. During the summer of 1858, 225 buildings, including 200 shops, were built. One colonist reported there could be a patch of green grass in the morning, and a house built on it by night.

In 1862, another steamship, *Brother Jonathan*, arrived from San Francisco. Along with pickaxes and gold pans, one miner carried deadly cargo—smallpox. Instead of widespread vaccinations and general quarantine, the colonial government forced the Indigenous people out of their camps at gunpoint and burned down their homes. This drove people out of town to spread the disease back to their communities. Smallpox was devastating to the Coastal First Nations. It is estimated that 20,000 Indigenous people died in this epidemic, about 60% of the population.

Many of the historical figures mentioned in this novel are legendary, and not only with British Columbia history buffs. Sir James Douglas was a prominent figure and became Governor of the new Colony of British Columbia in 1858. His wife, Lady Amelia Douglas, whose mother was Cree and father was Irish, was one of the colony's midwives, as portrayed in the novel.

The following historical figures had bit parts, cameos, or honorable mentions in *Wild Bird.* Matthew Begbie was a lawyer who came to the colony in 1858, and was soon appointed judge, and traveled miles on horseback to hear cases, holding court in saloons, roadhouses, or outdoors. One of the true "characters" of Victoria history was Amor De Cosmos who was a newspaper editor of *The British Colonist.* Born William Smith, he changed his name to mean "Love of the Cosmos" in Spanish. Augustus Frederick Pemberton was appointed commissioner of police for the colony of Vancouver Island in 1858. During the smallpox epidemic, he was responsible for removing indigenous people from town, expelling others from their encampments, and burning Indigenous migrants' lodgings. And finally, Dr. John Helmcken was employed by the Hudson's Bay Company in 1850 as a surgeon. In the novel, Dr. Harding's notes that Kate pored over were largely based on Helmcken's medical journal.

©Jennifer Callioux Photography

# Interview with Leanne Baugh

**What led you to want to tell Kate Harding's story?**
I have always been fascinated how women throughout history have bumped up against societal barriers to force change in society. Kate is a young woman wishing to become a physician, at a time when women were not welcomed into the profession. She educated herself, sacrificed, and made difficult choices, but she never lost sight of her dream. And with help from both Lucy and Rebecca, we know at the end of the novel that she was one step closer to fulfilling that dream. I hope, in some way, Kate's journey will be an inspiration for readers.

**Did you have aspirations to practice medicine when you were a young person?**
Yes, but my high school Math and Sciences marks determined my destiny. It was clear my academic strengths were in English

and Social Studies, which eventually led me to writing.

**Why did you choose to begin the story with the graphic scene of Mama giving birth to Violet?**

Giving birth in the nineteenth century was often perilous for both mother and baby. The grief that Kate had experienced over the death of her infant siblings was one of the underlying factors that propelled her interest in medicine. And attending Violet's birth initiated her curiosity.

**As you wrote this story and worked to make it authentic to the period in which it is set, how did this affect the language and style of the storytelling?**

Trying to get the "voice" right for this novel was a delicate balance. I wanted to capture both the storytelling style and formal language of the period, but also make it accessible to readers. How I prepared for this was to read or reread novels written in the 19th century, including *Jane Eyre*. As well, I watched many BBC period dramas set in the 19th century to hear the spoken language. After that research, the writing became easier.

**Although this is a work of historical fiction, set in a period 160 years ago, it has a lot of relevance for our times. Is that why you wanted to tell this story?**

I didn't purposefully set out to write this story based on its relevance to the present day. But there are some interesting parallels in terms of women's rights, the MeToo movement, Indigenous reconciliation, and now the COVID-19 pandemic that has recently hit our world.

**Having a curious mind, with a passion for reading, is something Kate values, above all. Why do you think that, despite the great leaps our society has taken since her time, she is still a character young people today can learn from?**

Kate does have a curious mind, and she's also feisty, intelligent, dutiful, compassionate, and, against all odds, she strives to realize her dream. I think these are qualities everyone, no matter what age, would benefit from developing.

**You are obviously fascinated by the time and place you have chosen for your story in this book. What would be your advice to young writers who might like to tell stories from another age?**

I was determined to write *Wild Bird* as historically authentic as possible. This led to much research: photocopying special collections in the Heritage Room at my local library; reading numerous books (fiction and non-fiction) and articles; meeting with members of the Songhees First Nation; digging into the B.C. Archives; and, of course, searching the Internet. My advice to young writers would be, do as much research as possible on the place and time period that interests you. Basically, immerse yourself in that world.

**Thank you, Leanne, for all your insights.**